THRAXAS
at the
RACES

Look out for these other Thraxas adventures
from Martin Scott

THRAXAS
THRAXAS AND THE WARRIOR MONKS

THRAXAS
at the
RACES

Martin Scott

ORBIT

An *Orbit* Book

First published in Great Britain by Orbit 1999

A CIP catalogue record for this book
is available from the British Library.

ISBN 1 85723 734 X

Typeset by Solidus (Bristol) Ltd, Bristol
Printed and bound in Great Britain by
Mackays of Chatham plc, Chatham, Kent

Orbit
A Division of
Little, Brown and Company (UK)
Brettenham House
Lancaster Place
London WC2E 7EN

CHAPTER
ONE

I step out of the law courts. It's still raining. A huge clap of thunder explodes in the sky. I growl with annoyance.

'Terrific. The judge just fined me everything I have left, it's the rainy season and now the storms have started.'

The sky is turning very ugly. My face is much the same. I can't remember being in a worse mood. Ex-Deputy Consul Rittius certainly managed to put one over on me this time. If I ever meet him in a dark alley, I'll skewer him with a rusty dagger. It won't even have to be dark. Any alley will do.

'You still have some money left,' says Makri.

'I lost a little at the out-of-town chariot races.'

'A little? How much?'

I shake my head, which Makri correctly interprets to mean everything I had. Lightning splits the sky. Rain starts pelting down harder than ever. A small, mean-faced figure emerges from the law courts, the white of his official toga showing under his fur-lined cloak. It's Senator Rittius, formerly Deputy Consul of Turai, and still head of Palace Security. He's flanked by eight Guards. I consider running him through anyway, but hold myself back.

He sticks his thin face close to mine. 'You were lucky, Thraxas,' he says, with loathing in his voice. 'The judge was far too lenient. If I had my way you'd be rowing a slave galley by now.'

'Really? If you bother me any more, ratface, you'll be handing in your toga way ahead of schedule.'

'Don't threaten me, fat man,' hisses Rittius. 'Or I'll have you back in court so fast it'll make you dizzy. I'm still head of Palace Security. You take one step outside the law and I'll be down on you like a bad spell. Your life in Turai is finished. I advise you to leave while you still can.'

I stare at Rittius with hatred. I did him a very bad turn a while back. In the course of an investigation last summer I seriously dented his political ambitions and caused him to lose the election for Deputy Consul. I still feel good about it.

'Stay out my way,' I tell him. 'Your Guard won't stop me gutting you if I get a notion to.'

My hand strays towards the sword at my hip. Rittius flinches, very slightly. He knows I could do it. He recovers himself quickly, and sneers at me.

'I think you'll find you've got far too much on your plate to go around inflicting violence on your betters,' he says.

Rittius departs. His Guards march after him through the rain in good order.

'You certainly know how to make influential friends,' says Makri. She offers to buy me a beer and we hurry through the ever increasing downpour to the tavern at the edge of the law courts where the accused steady their nerves before their ordeal and the barristers spend their fees afterwards.

'How long did you say this rain lasted?' asks Makri, who's only recently arrived in Turai, and has not yet become used to our seasons.

'A month. And it'll get worse now the storms have arrived. Last year Gurd had to shore up the walls of the Avenging Axe with sandbags.'

Makri and I live at the Avenging Axe, a tavern in Twelve Seas. It's not much of a place to live, but nowhere is in Twelve Seas, the rough area by the docks. It's the sort of place you end up if your life isn't going too well. Like for instance if you're a highly paid Senior Investigator working at the Imperial Palace who is booted out of his job for alleged drunkenness, insubordination and whatever else it was I was accused of.

Rittius was my boss back then. He hated me then and since I put one over on him last summer it's become even worse. I helped clear a Royal Princess's name as well as the son of Rittius's opponent of serious charges. Rittius promptly lost the election. I knew he'd be out to get me but I never thought he'd stoop so low as to use his position at the Palace to drag me through the courts accused of assaulting an officer of the law.

'What the hell was I supposed to do?' I complain as I sink my flagon of ale and hold it out for a refill. 'I needed that landus in a hurry. I could hardly stand around asking politely, could I? So I hauled the guy out and roughed him up a bit. I wasn't to know he was a Praetor's Assistant on a secret mission for the King. He wasn't even wearing an official toga.'

I'm seething with the injustice of it all.

'I thought I'd get through the Hot Rainy Season without having to work. I hate investigating in the rain. Now I'm broke I'll have to.'

Gurd, the ageing Barbarian who owns the Avenging Axe, is an old fighting companion. We were soldiers and mercenaries together. He tolerates a fair amount by having a Private Investigator like myself as a tenant. Only last month the place was practically wrecked when the Brotherhood, the local criminal gang, slugged it out with two bands of warrior monks in the downstairs bar. Gurd figures the least I can do is pay the rent on time. Which, until my unwise speculations on the recent out-of-town chariot races, I fully intended to do.

'Do you ever win at the races?'

'Of course, I win plenty.'

Makri scoffs. She claims she could find more winners at the chariot races than me by simply throwing a dart at the form sheet. I remind her that she's an ignorant Barbarian with Orc blood in her veins who's so unused to civilisation she still finds it awkward to use cutlery.

'Stick to what you're good at, Makri.'

'Like what?'

'Like killing people. You're good at that.'

Makri accepts the compliment. It's true enough. Since Makri escaped from the Orcs' gladiator slave pits last year and headed on over to civilisation, she's proved herself pretty much invincible with a sword in her hand. This has been of great benefit to me on several occasions when my investigations have got nasty. They often do. During the attack of the warrior monks Makri demonstrated her skills in such a savage and devastating manner that Captain Rallee was left shaking his head in amazement, and Captain Rallee has seen a lot of fighting in his time.

'But superior fighting skills count for nothing at the race track. The problem was that the out-of-town meeting was fixed. You can't trust the resident Sorcerers at these small events. Not like here in the city. With Melus the Fair as Stadium Sorcerer you know everything is above board. She's practically the only honest person in Turai. She ensures that magic is never used at the Stadium Superbius. But that small meeting was a joke. I swear the chariot that won the last race wouldn't have made it out of the stable without a spell to show the horses which way to go. I should have known better than to gamble on it. There again, I wasn't expecting Rittius to drag me into court the following week.'

'Could have been worse,' says Makri, paying for my third beer. 'You might be rowing a trireme by now. Rittius really hates you. How badly did you behave at his wedding anyway?'

'Pretty badly,' I admit. 'But if he wanted the guests to remain in order he shouldn't have provided so much free wine. That's strong stuff they ship up from the Elvish Islands. And his bride should have been better covered up. That dress was hardly modest.'

I stare gloomily at the bar. Since the unfortunate incident at the wedding, the last few years have been pretty rough. Now I'll have to find a case and investigate it. Damn it. I really hate working in the rainy season.

Outside rain pours down and thunder rumbles overhead. I notice a Sorcerer walking towards us, easily identifiable by his rainbow cloak. He's a large man with a weighty-looking staff in his hand. He stops in front of me and pulls back his hood revealing a pair of steely eyes and a square jaw line. My heart sinks. It's Glixius Dragon Killer. I thought he'd left town.

'I'm going to kill you, Thraxas,' he says, in his deep voice.

'What, right now? Or some other time when you've got nothing better to do?'

Glixius fixes me with his steely gaze for a second or two, then turns and marches off without another word.

Makri is shielding her eyes with her hand as if trying to pick out something on the horizon.

'What are you doing?'

'Seeing where the next deadly enemy is coming from.'

'Very funny. Rittius and now Glixius. Some day.'

Glixius Dragon Killer is a powerful Sorcerer associated with the Society of Friends, Turai's second major criminal organisation. Funnily enough, I did him a very bad turn this summer as well. It was a big summer for doing bad turns to powerful people. I foiled his plot to steal Red Elvish Cloth. I punched him in the face too, as I recall, though he was all out of magic at the time.

There isn't a landus to be found anywhere so we trudge home through the rain. I'm gloomier than ever. What a day. The state fines me all my money and two deadly enemies threaten me.

'It wouldn't be so bad if I ever made any profit out of this investigating business.'

'You do,' points out Makri. 'But you spend most of it on beer and gamble the rest away.'

Makri is a very hard worker. She works shifts as a barmaid at the Avenging Axe to pay for her classes at the Guild College. She's not above occasionally pointing out to me the error of my ways. Not that Makri doesn't have her share of faults. I strongly suspect that she's been experimenting with dwa, the powerful drug that has half the city in its grip, though she always denies it.

'Give me a turn with the magic dry cloak,' she says.

'No chance,' I reply. 'I need it more than you. If I'm about to get attacked by Palace Security and a deadly Sorcerer, I need to be comfortable.'

I wrap myself tighter in the magic dry cloak. Makri makes a face. It's odd. In her short life she's fought and defeated practically every kind of beast and warrior known and she will charge an impossible force of enemies without the slightest qualm, but she really detests getting wet.

'Damn this rain. At least it was dry in the gladiator slave pits,' she grumbles. 'I hate this Hot Rainy Season. How can it be hot as Orcish hell and wet as a Mermaid's blanket at the same time?'

She pulls her thin cloak over her vast mane of hair. If she's trying to make me feel guilty she's wasting her time. I didn't spend all that time studying sorcery to learn how to make a magic dry cloak just to hand it over to the first person that asks.

'Where are we going?' asks Makri, as I take a diversion down a series of twisting alleyways.

'I'm calling in at Honest Mox's.'

'Honest Mox the bookie? But the Stadium Superbius is shut in the rainy season.'

'There's a race meeting in Juval. It's dry there at this time of year.'

Juval is a small nation, another member of the League of City-States to which Turai belongs. It's a couple of hundred miles southeast of Turai. Makri wonders how I can bet on chariot races so far away. I explain to her that the bookmakers here band together to pay a Sorcerer to transmit messages to another Sorcerer at the race track in Juval. He sends up the runners and the prices and afterwards transmits the results. It's not an uncommon practice among gamblers in Turai to bet on these races. Makri is impressed, though somewhat surprised to find Sorcerers engaged in such practices.

'I thought they all concerned themselves with higher callings.'

'Well, mainly young Apprentices take the work. The Sorcerers Guild doesn't really approve but, hey, it's good practice for sending messages, which is handy in wartime.'

'Haven't you lost enough recently?'

'That's why I have to win it back. I have an emergency supply for just this situation.'

Mox the bookmaker is, as ever, pleased to see me. He's chalked the runners in the next race in Juval up on a board. I study the form.

'How do you know the Sorcerers transmit everything honestly?' asks Makri.

I admit that this can be a worry. Race Sorcerers have been know to be dishonest, but it's a risk I'm prepared to take. I've never had any trouble with the meeting in Juval. It's a small track, usually with only four chariots in each race. I can't see anything beating the favourite, a fine chariot from Samsarina called Glorious Warrior. It's only even money so I place twenty gurans on it.

'You're wasting your money,' sniffs Makri.

'Oh, yes? You won't say that when I pick up my twenty gurans winnings tomorrow.'

CHAPTER
TWO

We trudge on down Moon and Stars Boulevard till we reach Twelve Seas. Around the law courts the rain was bouncing off the statues of past kings and heroes of Turai, running down the marble pavements into the well-maintained gutters. In the smarter parts of Turai public utilities such as drainage are a marvel of engineering. Not so in Twelve Seas. Here the downpour turns the dirt streets to mud. After ten days of rain the place looks pretty bad. Another twenty to go. Twelve Seas is hell in the Hot Rainy Season.

'My shift starts in two minutes and I'm wet as a Mermaid's blanket,' complains Makri, and hurries off to change.

I climb the outside stairs leading directly from Quintessence Street into my office above the tavern. There's a sign outside my door: *Finest Sorcerous Investigator in the City of Turai*. The rain is starting to peel off the paint where it flaked in the burning summer sun. Sorcerous Investigator. Big joke. I studied as an Apprentice but that was a long time ago. Now my powers are of the lowest grade, mere tricks compared with the skills of Turai's great Wizards.

I should do something about that sign. It looks cheap. I'm probably the cheapest Sorcerous Investigator in the whole of Turai but there's no need to brag about it. I'm forty-three, overweight, without ambition, prone to prolonged bouts of drinking and I take on the sort of case the Civil Guards won't help with for the sort of client that can't afford one of the high-class Investigators uptown. I charge ten gurans a day plus expenses which is never going to make me rich.

Things were looking up. This summer I solved a couple of important cases, earned myself a fair bit of reward money, improved my reputation in certain important circles. With a bit of luck I might have made it out of Twelve Seas back into proper society again. Now that I've been dragged through the courts on a charge of assaulting an official of the King, I'm back at square one. No money, and no reputation.

The atmosphere is cloying. The Hot Rainy Season is unbearable. It's like a steam bath out there. If it wasn't for my magic dry cloak I don't think I could cope. As my magic is so poor nowadays, I can generally only carry one or two spells around at a time. Usually I take a sleep spell, which is highly effective in rendering opponents unconscious, and maybe something like a loud explosion to cause a diversion. The days when I could work invisibility and levitation are long gone. Right now my entire sorcerous ability is concentrated on keeping dry. If I happen to meet five or six opponents at once I'll just have to rely on my sword.

My office is a mess. I kick some junk under the table, grab a beer from the supply in the sink and drop down on the couch muttering a few oaths about the unfairness of life. I fought for this damned city in the last Orc Wars. Helped throw back the savage horde that threatened to overwhelm us from the east. Not to mention the sterling service I gave the city in the war before that, with Nioj, when our enemies from the north swept through the mountain passes and damn near threw us all into the sea. And is anyone grateful? No chance. To hell with them all.

There's a knock on the outside door.

'To hell with you all,' I shout.

The knock comes again. I'm in no mood for company. I shout out another curse, finish my beer and prepare to toss the bottle at the doorframe. The door opens and in walks Senator Mursius, one of Turai's greatest war heroes and my old commander from the Army. He's tall, erect, silver-haired and extremely vigorous-looking for a man of fifty. Pretty angry-looking as well.

'What is the meaning of this?' he demands in a voice that takes me straight back to the parade ground. 'I am not accustomed to former soldiers treating me with disrespect.'

I scramble to my feet. Senator Mursius was the last person I expected to walk into my office. Great heroes of Turai tend not to visit. It must be fifteen years since we last spoke, probably around the time when the platoon commanded by Mursius was holding out at a breach in our walls made by the besieging Orc Army, and I was one of the unfortunate soldiers forming a human shield to keep them at bay. I've seen him since of course, in one of the galleries reserved for Senators at the theatre or the Stadium Superbius, but I doubt if he ever noticed me.

Now he's noticed, he's not looking too impressed.

'You always were a disgusting apology for a soldier,' he barks. 'I see that time hasn't improved you.'

Mursius is still a big man and he wears his white sena-
torial toga with a majestic air. I'm only in my underwear,
which probably isn't helping things. I struggle back into
my tunic and clear some junk from a chair.

'Won't you sit down, Senator Mursius?'

'You've put on a lot of weight,' he says, eyeing my
girth with the sort of disapproving gaze he used to
reserve for ill-attired recruits. 'And you've come down in
the world.'

He knows all about my fall from grace. He's not
unsympathetic. As a soldier he has little time for Palace
politics.

'A vipers' nest, the Palace. You should never have
taken a job there in the first place. Why did you do it?'

'The pay was good.'

'Look where it got you.'

He looks around my shabby room. 'Did Rittius clean
you out in court?'

I nod.

'Rittius is a snake. Never did a day's fighting in his life.
That's the sort of person who's running Turai these
days. I take it you are looking for work?'

I nod again.

'I need the services of an Investigator. Nothing too
complicated, or so I believe. I'd normally have hired a
man closer to home, but I thought you might be in need
of employment.'

I ask him why exactly he thought that and he replies
that he keeps an eye on most of the men who fought
under him.

'You weren't too bad that day at the walls, Thraxas.
I'd be sorry to see you starve. Though I see that would

take a while. I hear you have a reputation as a good Investigator. When you can stay sober. How often can you stay sober?'

'Practically all the time if the case really calls for it.'

A knock comes on the inner door that leads downstairs into the tavern. It opens before I get the chance to answer it. Makri has little concept of personal privacy. You have to make allowances for her. She grew up in a slave pit, after all.

For the first time Mursius shows some surprise. Makri can be a surprising sight if you're not prepared for it. Though only slightly taller than your average Turanian woman, she carries herself erect like a warrior, lithe and strong like a fierce chagra cat from the Simnian jungle. She has large dark eyes, almost black, a huge mane of dark hair and strikingly attractive features, but what usually impresses anyone visiting the Avenging Axe for the first time is Makri's shape. Makri has plenty of shape – and her shape is difficult to miss given the tiny chainmail bikini she wears while working as a barmaid. The purpose of this of course is to earn tips from the dockers, sailors and mercenaries who make up most of Gurd's clientele.

The next thing people generally notice about Makri is the reddish, slightly dark hue of her skin. Makri is one quarter Orc, and that means trouble. She's quarter Elf as well, which is fine in Turai, where everyone likes Elves, but the Orc blood leads to all sorts of difficulties. Everyone in Turai hates the Orcs. Though we are technically at peace with them now and have even signed a treaty and swapped Ambassadors, you don't need too long a memory to recall the days when they were besieging the city.

All of which means that Makri's Orc blood is bad news in Turai. The drinkers in the tavern are fairly used to it but Makri still wouldn't be allowed into a high-class tavern up town, or various official buildings. She is often insulted in the street. I'd worry about her more if it wasn't for the fact that she's probably the most lethal fighter in Turai, if not the entire west. I've spent most of my life fighting, and I can't recall ever meeting anyone more deadly with a sword, an axe, or anything that comes to hand.

Senator Mursius stares at her in surprise. There is an awkward silence.

'I've got pointed ears as well,' says Makri, which is true, though they're usually hidden beneath her huge mass of hair.

'Excuse me,' says the Senator apologetically. He glances at the sword at her hip. 'An Orc blade?'

Makri nods. 'I brought it with me.'

Mursius looks at it with interest. As a professional soldier he always was interested in weaponry.

'Fine work,' he says with approval. 'The Orcs are excellent armourers, whatever people say. Quite as good as the best Human smiths. You say you brought it with you?'

'From the Orc gladiator pits. I used to fight there. Before I killed the Orc Lord who owned me, slaughtered his entourage, escaped down a sheer cliff face and took a job as a barmaid instead.'

'Interesting. Your attire seems hardly suitable for fighting, however.'

'You're right,' agrees Makri. 'Only a fool would go fighting in a bikini. But it gets me tips. When I'm on duty

I hide the sword behind the bar.' She departs downstairs.

'A very interesting woman,' says Mursius. 'Half Orc?'

'A quarter. Quarter Elf as well. And half Human, though that doesn't make her act like one.'

The Senator studies me with interest. He's wondering if he wants to hire an Investigator who's having a relationship with a quarter Orc. He needn't worry. I'm not having a relationship with Makri, or anyone else for that matter. Haven't had one for a long time. I went off women when my wife left me for a young Sorcerer's Apprentice some years ago. I took to drink instead. Actually I had taken to drink some time before she left, but afterwards I had much more time for it.

'So, how can I help you?'

The Senator tells me that he has suffered from a theft at his country house further down the coast, near to Ferai. Like any wealthy citizen, the Senator keeps a house in town and another in the country for retiring to when the weather gets too intense.

'My losses are not great. There wasn't much money at the villa, but various works of art have gone missing and I'd like them recovered. In particular I'd like you to find a painting which I hold very dear.'

Remembering Mursius in his younger days, storming the Orc lines with a bloody sword in his hand, I never figured him as an art lover. You can never tell with these aristocrats, though. Men of Mursius's generation went naturally into war and fought bravely, but they learned their share of social graces as well. There used to be a theory among the aristocratic class that it was important to enrich every aspect of one's personality. But Turai was different in those days. Since the gold mines in the north started producing wealth and the drug trade brought dwa in from the south, the city is both much richer and much more corrupt. Today's young aristocrats spend their time in debauchery and bribe their way out of military service.

'What have the Civil Guards done about it?'

'I have not informed them.'

I raise one eyebrow. Calling in the Guards would be the normal thing to do, unless there was some delicate aspect Mursius would rather not reveal in public. I was half expecting something like this. People do tend to come to me only in desperate circumstances.

'I have not informed them,' continues Mursius, 'because I strongly suspect that my wife was behind the theft.'

'Your wife?'

The Senator expresses some anxiety about the private nature of his disclosures. I reassure him of my discretion. I have plenty of faults but I never blab about a client, even if it gets me thrown in jail. Which it does, often enough.

Outside the rain beats against the shutters, drowning out the other noise from the street. That's the only good thing about the Hot Rainy Season. It keeps most of the squealing brats that infest the area indoors.

'We have been estranged for some time. We stay together because it suits us not to part. I'm sure you understand.'

I do. For a city as immoral as Turai, where almost everyone can be bought, the public still places a surprisingly high value on the morality of our public figures. If a Senator finds himself involved in a messy divorce case it can do great damage to his career and completely end his chances of advancing up the ladder of Prefect, Praetor, Deputy Consul and Consul. They tend to keep their problems hushed up and well away from the scandal sheets. Their wives generally go along with it. It suits them better to remain married and keep their wealth and social standing rather than risk finding themselves out on the market again.'

'So, why would she rob you?'

'My wife is often desperate for money.'

'You don't give her an allowance?'

'Not for dwa, no.'

Right. Not for dwa. That makes sense. Since the southern trade routes were opened up, this powerful narcotic has flooded into the city. The effect on the population has been dramatic. Beggars, sailors, youthful apprentices, whores, itinerants, rich young things: all manner of people once content to alleviate their sufferings with ale and occasional doses of the much milder drug thazis now spend their days lost in the powerful dreams of dwa. Unfortunately dwa is both expensive and addictive. Once you take your dose you're as happy as an Elf in a tree, but when you come down you feel bad. Regular users who spend part of their lives lost in its pleasant grip are obliged to spend the other part raising money for more.

Since dwa swept Turai, crime has accelerated out of control. In many parts of Turai it's not safe to walk the streets at night for fear of violent robbery. The city is rotting. The poor are despairing and the rich are decadent. One day King Lamachus of Nioj will come down from the north and sweep us away.

'Is she a serious addict?'

'Very serious. She's tried to stop but—'

He holds his hands out in a hopeless gesture.

'For the past six months she's been down at the villa. It was her idea. Said it would help her to get straight. From what the servants tell me, it hasn't worked out. I've tried doctors, Sorcerers, herbalists, everything. Nothing does any good. She always comes back to dwa. Eventually I tried cutting off her money, just sending down a servant with supplies.'

'As a result of which your wife sold some of the family treasures to feed her habit?'

'So it would seem.'

I lean back in my chair and take a thazis stick from my drawer. I offer one to the Senator, but he declines. It's still technically illegal but since the arrival of dwa swept the city no one much cares about that. I light it up and inhale the smoke.

'What exactly do you want me to do?'

'Find my belongings. Particularly the painting. Without involving the Guard or the scandal sheets.'

The Senator tells me in a frank, man-to-man sort of way that he's being pressed by the Traditionals to stand for the post of Prefect next year. He's fifty years old so it's about time for his political career to get started. As a war hero and a popular man with both the mob and the King, he's almost certain to get elected. Unless, of course, his name is blackened by scandal. The Populares, the powerful opposition party led by Senator Lodius, never hesitate to use any available dirt against their opponents.

I mull it over. It means travelling out of the city in the rain, which is a fairly unpleasant prospect with the country turning into swampland, but apart from that it sounds straightforward enough. No powerful criminal gangs involved. No mad Sorcerers out to get me. Just find out what she did with the goods and get them back. I can do that. I need the money. I take the case.

The Senator fills me in on the rest of the details and rises from his chair. He pauses at the door and glances round the room. 'I hear you lost a great deal of money at the out-of-town chariot meeting.'

I frown. I knew the Senator would have checked me out but a man never likes his gambling losses being made too public.

'I'll give you a good tip for the Turas Memorial Race.'

I lean forward, suddenly eager.

'I'm entering a chariot in the Turas Memorial,' says the Senator. 'It's called Storm the Citadel. Back it. It's going to win.'

I sit back, disappointed. I'm not too keen on this tip.

'Your chariot is going to win the Turas Memorial Race? Excuse me, Senator, you've had some good horse teams in the past, but there's an Elvish entrant in the Turas this year. Everyone knows Moonlit River is going to win. You can't even get a bet down on it any more.'

The Senator treads softly back to my desk. 'Storm the Citadel will win,' he says, quite emphatically. 'If you want to make up your losses, back it with everything you have.'

With that he departs. I pick up a guran from the retainer he left me and head downstairs to the bar where I buy a flagon of Gurd's finest ale and muse about Senators' wives and the powerful addictive qualities of dwa. I tried it when I was younger, but it didn't do much for me. I guess I'm just not that sort of character. I finish my beer quickly, drink down another, and take a third flagon back up to my office.

There's a message on my desk. Odd. I break the seal and open it. It reads: *Thraxas, your death is near.*

I stare at it. I'm used to death threats but that doesn't mean I enjoy them. I check the outside door. It's locked. I'm sure no one came up the connecting stairs while I was at the bar. I put the letter under my nose, sensing around for any signs of sorcery. Is there a faint trace? Possibly.

My hand goes automatically to the spell protection charm at my throat. It's new. I hope it works.

I'm wary as I travel out to Mox's, but when I find that my chariot won and I pick up my twenty gurans winnings, I forget about the death threat. Afterwards I gloat to Makri.

'Yes, a man may have a few losses every now and then, but class will tell in the end. When it comes to picking winners I'm number one chariot around here. And I've a hot tip for tomorrow. You ought to join in and win a little money, Makri. Easier than working as a waitress.'

CHAPTER
THREE

'What do you think of Storm the Citadel's chances in the Turas Memorial Race?' I ask Gurd as he hands me another beer. His biceps bulge as he passes it over the bar. His long hair is almost completely grey now but he's still as strong as a team of oxen.

'No chance,' he says. 'The Elves don't send a chariot all the way up from the Southern Islands unless they know it'll win.'

I nod. That's what everyone in Turai thinks. Senator Mursius has produced some fine chariots in his time, but he's never going to beat the Elves.

Everyone is looking forward to the chariot races in the dry week after the rains stop, when the Turas Festival is held. Turas was the legendary founder of Turai, building a city after defeating several savage tribes and performing various heroic acts. It's always a good time for Turai. It cheers up the citizens before the onset of the bitter winter. This year the festivities will take on a larger scale than usual because they come at the time of the Triple-Moon conjunction festival, which only happens every fifteen years or so.

I'll be betting at the meeting, naturally, but I hadn't planned putting anything on the last and most prestigious event, the Turas Memorial Race. Not with the Elves entering Moonlit River. It's practically a shoo-in. The chariot belongs to Lisith-ar-Moh, a great Elvish Lord and a particular friend of Turai. Fifteen years ago Lisith-ar-Moh led a regiment of Elvish warriors through the Orc lines to the relief of Turai, arriving just as the Orcs breached our walls and various desperate Turanian soldiers, including myself, were trying to hold them back. He saved the city that day and we have never forgotten it. He's visited several times since, as guest of honour to our King, and it's because of his ties with the city that he's entered a chariot in the Turas Memorial Race.

Everyone is pleased about that. We all like Elves here. The only thing wrong is that the Elvish chariot has more or less finished the Turas Memorial as a serious competition. We don't breed horses up here the way the Elves do in the Southern Islands.

And yet . . . like any gambler I'm always interested when someone gives me a tip. I stood beside Senator Mursius when the east wall of the city was breached and watched him fight hand to hand with the savage Orcish force swarming over the debris and into the city. If Mursius hadn't been there to lead us we'd never have held out till the Elves arrived.

'He's not the sort of man to place his faith in a no-hoper,' I point out to Gurd, who was there that day as well.

'True. But chariot-owners always think they're going to win,' replies Gurd. 'You've lost plenty at the races already. No point throwing more away.'

Gurd and I reminisce about the war. We've done that often recently. The imminent arrival of Lord Lisith has certainly stirred up the memories. Orcs, dragons, walls

tumbling to the ground under sorcerous attack, buildings on fire, the desperate battle, the sound of trumpets
and the sudden unexpected arrival of the Elves. Even
when they arrived it was no easy matter to defeat the
Orcs. The fight continued all day and all night and all of
the next day as well. It was quite an experience. So I
figure Gurd and I are fully justified in bragging about our
part in it, no matter what anyone might say when we
wheel out our war stories for another airing.

Gurd is right about the race of course. And yet . . .
Mursius is sharp as an Elf's ear when it comes to chariot
racing. He's had a lot of success. I can feel myself being
tempted. I banish it from my mind and get back to the
task in hand, namely recovering Senator Mursius's lost
works of art. Gurd has a couple of good horses out the
back and I ask the stable lad to saddle one of them up for
me while Tanrose, the tavern cook and object of Gurd's
Barbarian affections, fills me a basket of provisions for
the journey. I tie back my long hair and tuck it inside my
tunic, then wrap myself in my cloak.

Just as I'm leaving Makri enters the tavern.

'I'm wet as a Mermaid's blanket,' she states. 'What a
stupid climate this city has. If it isn't too hot, it's too wet.
Now it's both.'

I have to agree. The weather in Turai is often unpleasant. We have four months of blazing sun, one month of
hot rain, about one month of a fairly temperate autumn,
then four months of extreme, biting cold. After that
there's another rainy season, cold this time, lasting a
month, before the month-long spring, which is pleasant.

'Which makes only two reasonable months a year,'
growls Makri.

'At least it's regular.'

'Why the hell did anyone ever build a city here?'

'Good harbour. And we're on the main trade routes.'

Makri curses in archaic Elvish. She's been learning the Royal Elvish language at her Guild classes and wants to practise.

'Not that the Elves ever curse the rain, or so I'm told,' continues Makri. 'Apparently they all sit around in their trees thinking it's yet another fine part of nature. Stupid Elves.'

Makri was already fluent in Common Elvish when she arrived in Turai. Presumably that was from her Elvish grandparent, but who that was I've never asked, and Makri has never exactly explained. Nor has she talked about her Orcish grandparent. I wouldn't dare ask. Anyway, both my Elvish and Orcish have improved a lot since she's been around.

I ask her what she was doing wandering around in the rain. She tells me she was looking for plants.

'What for?'

'Natural history class at the Guild College. The Professor wants us all to study some interesting local plants.'

'That might be difficult in Twelve Seas. There aren't any.'

'I know. I went to look in that small park behind Saint Rominius's Lane. Unfortunately the park's disappeared. Someone built a block of tenements right over it.'

King Reeth-Akan lays down strict regulations concerning the number of parks for his subjects. Even the poorest of areas should have open spaces for the citizenry to take their exercise and forget their cares for a while. Unfortunately the Prefects who control planning in each district are very amenable to looking the other way if bribed by property developers. It's reached the stage now where there's hardly an open space left in Twelve Seas. The last Prefect, Tholius, was as corrupt as they come. He was recently forced to flee the city after being caught out trying to divert some of the King's gold into his own coffers. Obviously Drinius, his replacement, hasn't wasted any time in lining his own pockets. You can tell a man of aristocratic birth because his name ends in 'ius'. But you could work it out anyway by his amazing willingness to take money for favours. 'Easy as bribing a Senator,' as they say. Not like the solid working-class citizens, who tend to have 'ox' or 'ax' in their names. Like Thraxas, for instance. They're as honest as they come.

'I'm just heading off into the country,' I tell Makri. 'Come along and study the plant life.'

Makri considers it. She has got the rest of the day free and she thinks she could use some exercise.

'Okay, I'll come along if I can share the magic dry cloak,' she says, cunningly. 'I need some interesting kind of plant. If I fail on this assignment Professor Toarius will be down on me like a bad spell.'

Makri scowls. From her frequent complaints I know that Professor Toarius is high on the long list of people associated with the Guild College who think it would be a far better place if it didn't include Makri. It was him who forbade her to attend classes in her chainmail bikini because of the disturbance she was creating Even the man's tunic she put over it didn't satisfy him.

'He said it showed too much of my thighs. Is that taboo in Turai?'

'No. Just distracting for young men trying to study philosophy.'

As a result of which she now has to wrap herself up in a voluminous cloak before going to college, even when the sun is beating down and it's hot as Orcish hell, which it was all summer.

'Professor Toarius is as cold as an Orc's heart,' grumbles Makri, and goes upstairs to get her axe.

Makri sticks at it though. She works hard, at the tavern and at the Guild College for the Education of the Sons of the Lower Classes. It's her ambition to go to the Imperial University. This, as I have frequently pointed out, is impossible. The University doesn't accept female students, especially ones with Orc blood in their veins. The Imperial University is such an exclusive institution, catering only for the offspring of aristocrats, that even our richest merchants have trouble getting their children in. It is a symbol of the complete control exercised by the ruling elite, which makes it even more impossible for Makri ever to attend. She refuses to be put off. 'The Guild College didn't take female students either before I insisted,' she points out. You have to admire her persistence.

She arrives back with her axe, two swords, a knife in her boot and a bag of throwing stars, an Assassins Guild weapon she's been experimenting with recently.

'Makri, you're only looking for a few plants. What the hell are you expecting to meet out there?'

'You never know. Any time I'm helping you on a case it always turns out worse than we expect. I still haven't forgotten the time we went looking for that missing dog and ended up fighting pirates. And look what happened the last time you made me go out without my axe. I ended up with a crossbow bolt in the chest and nearly died.'

'And we'd have missed you terribly. Let's go.'

'I found this envelope addressed to you on the stairs.'

I rip it open.

You'll never make it past the Hot Rainy Season, says the message.

'Another death threat?'

I nod. I should have killed Glixius Dragon Killer when I had the chance.

Outside it's still hot. The rain has intensified and my old cloak keeps me dry for about thirty seconds. Meanwhile Makri is comfortably wrapped up in the magic dry cloak.

'The rain doesn't seem so bad when you get used to it,' she says. 'Where are we going?'

'Ferias. An exclusive little resort further down the coast.'

'Then why aren't we heading for the west gate?'

'I'm calling in at Mox's. I have a hot tip.'

Makri nods. She might not approve of betting but she was impressed when she saw me come home with a twenty-guran profit.

Mox's small, dingy premises is full of punters in the damp and grubby tunics and cloaks worn by the common Turanian masses. Most of the lower classes, including myself, wear grey. A few of the more adventurous youngsters might burst into colour occasionally but exotic clothes are beyond the budget of most people. Only the upper classes wear white.

A messenger arrives every now and then with the

latest news from the Sorcerer at the track, hundreds of miles away in Juval. I'm here to bet on the first race tomorrow, just in case I don't make it back to the city tonight. Though I'm careful not to reveal anything I'm practically beside myself with glee. I've been looking forward to this race for a long time. It's my insurance policy.

The odds on the four chariots in the race are even money, six to four, six to one and eight to one. As a serious gambler I am not a man to throw away his cash on outsiders but I happen to know that Troll Mangler at six to one has a particularly good chance in this race. I whisper in Makri's ear.

'I know the owner, I was drinking with him just before he went south. He's been keeping this chariot in reserve, well out of sight. He told me he's never trained a better team of horses. That's why he's gone down to Juval, where he isn't known. He's going to make a bundle at six to one, and so am I.'

Mox is slightly surprised when I confidently place forty gurans on Troll Mangler. Outside I do a little jig in the rain.

'Two hundred and forty gurans to Thraxas, thank you very much.'

'What if it loses?' says Makri as she swings herself on to her horse.

'No chance. Trust me. I know what I'm doing.'

The thunderstorm has passed but there will be plenty more of them in the month to come. It's a two-hour ride down the coast to Ferias. By the time we reach the city walls my good humour at placing the bet has disappeared and I'm starting to regret taking this case.

When we're halfway there I seriously consider turning back.

'This is grim,' I splutter. 'I'm about as miserable as a Niojan whore. I haven't been this wet since Gurd and I swam underneath an enemy raft in the war against the Niojans and attacked them by surprise. And I was a lot younger then.'

We stop for something to eat, sheltering under a tree. Makri looks around for some interesting plant life.

'I have to turn up with something really special. All I can see here is grass and bushes.'

'They'll probably have some unusual plants in the grounds at Mursius's villa. Steal one of them.'

We ride on.

'What are you meant to do when you get there? Isn't his wife going to find it rather offensive if you just march in and demand to know what she did with the loot?'

I look at Makri with interest. When she arrived in Turai I don't think she understood the concept of being offensive. The classes must be civilising her.

'Maybe. But Mursius doesn't care. Their relationship has passed the point of being polite. He just wants his paintings back.'

The rain lashes down. I swear a few curses at Rittius. If he hadn't dragged me through the courts I wouldn't have to be doing this. Thank God he's not Deputy Consul any more. That post is now occupied by Cicerius, who belongs to the Traditionals, the party that supports the King. They'd been losing ground to the opposition Populares but Cicerius's victory stemmed the tide. I had a hand in the victory. Thanks to some smart work on my part Cicerius avoided losing his reputation. Not that I particularly support the Traditionals. The Populares have some things in their favour. The common people could do with a little more of the city's wealth. Unfortunately the Populares are led by Senator Lodius, as nakedly ambitious a tyrant as ever put on a toga.

'How come Cicerius didn't use his influence to protect you in court?' asks Makri. 'After all, he's Deputy Consul now, and he owes you a favour.'

That's a very sore point. First thing I did when the trouble arose was visit Cicerius but he would have to be the one man in Turai who is both absolutely incorruptible and a sworn upholder of the law. He expressed sympathy for my plight, but refused to use his influence to get the charges thrown out. Because, as he pointed out in his beautifully modulated orator's voice, I was actually guilty. I had dragged the King's representative from his landus and bludgeoned him to the ground. The fact that I needed the vehicle urgently was not, in Cicerius's considered legal opinion, a valid defence for roughing up a fellow citizen.

'Trust you to gain influence with the one official too honest to bend the rules in your favour.'

We're now approaching the loose collection of large country dwellings that make up Ferias. Progress is slow. The ground is churned up and muddy and several streams have swollen, so it's difficult to get across. It's a long time since I've been here. When I was Senior Investigator at the Palace I visited regularly as the guest of various Senators, Praetors and wealthy Sorcerers. Now I'm about as welcome as an Orc at an Elvish wedding.

It's now well into the afternoon. My mood gets worse.

The rain comes down in huge drops. After two hours it feels like rocks pounding on my head. I tell Makri it's my turn for the cloak and we swap over.

'If you were any good as a Sorcerer you could make two of them.'

'If I was any good as a Sorcerer I wouldn't be here. I'd be safe in a big villa in Thamlin casting horoscopes for Princesses and courtiers and generally having an easy time of it. I should have studied more when I was an Apprentice.'

We mount a small hill and there in the distance is Mursius's villa. Suddenly my horse whinnies and rears up. I struggle to regain control but the wet reins fly from my hands and I plunge to the ground. I struggle to my feet, sliding in the mud and cursing freely at the ignorant beast. Without warning three large Orcs with swords step out from behind the nearest tree.

CHAPTER
FOUR

This doesn't make sense. You don't find Orcs in the Human Lands. Especially not in the excessively wealthy settlement of Ferias.

Orcs are larger than Humans, and generally a little stronger. I never met one that wasn't fierce, though as I've only met them on the battlefield, I suppose some might not be. Maybe the Orc poets all stay at home. I doubt it. Most Humans regard them as dumb animals but I haven't found that to be true. Their Ambassadors, for instance, have often proved to be shrewd negotiators, and Bhergaz the Fierce, the Great Orc leader of fifteen years ago who united all the Orcish nations and led them into the west, was a brilliant general. Only through a combination of luck, sorcery and desperation were the combined forces of Elves and Humans able to defeat him.

Makri hates them more fiercely than anyone. Despite this she refuses to acknowledge that Human civilisation is more advanced. She claims that contrary to what is believed in the west, Orcs do have music, literature and even a theatre of sorts, with extended performances of various religious rituals. If this is true, it's completely unknown to us, apart from the savage martial tunes they play when advancing into battle and the weird, shrieking pipe music they play from the backs of their dragons. Orcs can breed and control dragons, Humans can't. They're dark-skinned and wear their hair long, a style favoured by only the lower classes in Turai, and they dress in shaggy, tasselled black clothes. They're fond of silver jewellery. They make good weapons. They hate all Humans. And they can fight. So can I, which is fortunate as I'm not carrying any spells. I whip out my sword and my dagger and sink into my fighting stance.

The three Orcs are in the garb of young warriors, with black helmets and tunics and weapons at their hips. But they haven't attacked us yet. Strange. Orcs and Humans are implacable enemies. We waste no time when we meet. We just kill each other. I wonder if it might be worth asking them what they're doing here.

I don't get the chance. Makri's hatred of Orcs doesn't allow for conversation. With a decisive movement she rides one of them down and leaps off her horse to confront the others. Her axe and her sword are in her hands as she hits the ground and the first Orc's head flies from his shoulders before he has time to move. The second tries to draw his sword but Makri guts him and he slumps dead to the ground. I'm not the sort of man to let my companion fight on her own but I don't have the chance to join in. As the third Orc climbs to his feet Makri whips out a throwing star from her bag and tosses it with deadly accuracy right into his throat.

It's all over in seconds. Three dead Orcs lie sprawled at our feet. Seven years in the Orc gladiator pits, five of them as Supreme Champion, make a woman hard to beat.

Makri stalks around suspiciously, peering through the rain and sniffing the air for other Orcs.

There don't seem to be any more. There shouldn't have been any here in the first place. The Orcish nations are far away to the east. They don't wander around at will in the Human Lands. Any movement by a force of Orcs across the Wastelands that separate us would be detected by Human Sorcerers who scan continuously for just this sort of thing.

I wonder what they were doing here. There was something odd about their behaviour. We mount up and hurry on. A long white wall surrounds Mursius's villa. A heavy iron gate guards the front, behind which sits a bored-looking member of the Securitus Guild. I tell him my name and he nods as if expecting me. He opens the gate, and we ride in. When I tell him about the Orcs he looks at me with utter disbelief. I assure him it's true.

'Three warrior Orcs. Just up the hill. We dispatched them. You'd better have the local militia scour the area in case there's more.'

Realising that I'm serious, he hurries away to raise the alarm while Makri and myself head towards the house. The villa's extensive gardens are partially submerged after the weeks of rain. Two servants take our mounts off to the stables.

The experience with the Orcs hasn't put me off my mission. I have a living to earn. My instructions from Mursius are to talk to his wife and find out what she did with the works of art she sold. He didn't require me to be subtle about it, and I'm not planning to be. Just a few quick questions, find out where the loot is, then recover it.

My plan for a few quick questions goes wrong right away when a well-spoken young woman informs me that Sarija, Mursius's wife, can't see anybody just now.

I wave this away.

'Mursius sent me.'

'I know,' she replies. 'But you can't see her.'

'Why not?'

'She's unconscious from dwa.'

I stare at the young woman in surprise. One might have expected something more subtle.

She shrugs. 'It's the truth. I'm only paid to look after her, not tell lies.'

I get the strong impression that she's had more than enough of taking care of Sarija.

'If you want to wait she'll probably recover in a few hours. You can dry yourself in the guest rooms. I'll have a servant bring you some refreshment.'

The young woman's name is Carilis. She is pretty, in a bland sort of way. She speaks with the cultured voice of Turai's elite and is rather expensively dressed in one of these long white gowns they charge a fortune for in the market. She was obviously disconcerted by Makri's appearance. I wonder why she's playing nursemaid to a Senator's wife.

Shortly afterwards I'm drying myself in front of a fire as Makri roots around in the extensive window boxes decorating the large bay window. There's a tray of food in front of us and a flagon of wine on the table. We wait for a while, which is okay with me. I charge by the hour and if a few of these hours involve sitting around eating and drinking I'm not going to complain. I've just begun to feel comfortable when the door opens and a woman walks in. She is as white as a ghost and just about as healthy-looking.

'I'm Sarija,' she says. 'And it's time for you to get the hell out of my house.'

She picks up the flagon of wine. For a second I think she's about to throw it at me – Senators' wives are notoriously bad-tempered – but instead she puts it to her lips and pours a healthy slug down her throat. She coughs violently, throws up on a very expensive-looking rug then keels over unconscious.

We stare at her body, prostrate on the floor in a pool of wine, vomit and broken glass.

'I'll never really fit in with polite society,' says Makri.

I shake my head. 'Senators' wives. They get worse every year.'

I think about helping her up but I'm not really in the mood. I stride out into the corridor and holler for someone to come and help. Round the corner marches an Army Captain with eight armed men at his back. That's more help than I was really expecting. They're accompanied by the gatekeeper.

'He's the one.'

The Captain wears a red tunic covered by a silver breastplate. He's extremely wet and doesn't look friendly.

'What's the idea of sending me on a fool's errand looking for Orcs?' he demands.

I explain to him that it was not a fool's errand. The Orcs were there and Makri killed them.

'Makri?'

I lead him into the room. When confronted by a Senator's wife lying stretched out on the floor and a young woman in a chainmail bikini with an axe slung over her shoulder, the Captain becomes even more agitated.

'What the hell is going on here?' he demands.

'Just looking,' says Makri, and shifts around rather furtively.

'Don't worry,' I tell her. 'They haven't come about the plants.'

The Captain strides over to Sarija. I'm thinking that we might have some awkward explaining to do but fortunately at that moment Carilis appears. The Captain seems to know her and makes no comment as she attends to the Senator's wife. He turns back to me.

'Well?'

'We're down here on business at the request of Senator Mursius. And we met some Orcs. Didn't you find the bodies?'

He didn't. Nor did he find any trace of a fight. Not even a footprint.

'The rain must have washed it all away.'

'Very convenient. And would the rain also wash their aura away?'

'No, it wouldn't.'

'Well, we went there with a Sorcerer. A very important local man. He wasn't at all pleased to have the Army dragging him outdoors on a day like this. He was just settling down with a glass of wine and a new book of spells. But we told him it was important. A sudden appearance of Orcs.' The Captain fixes me with a grim stare. 'The Sorcerer couldn't find any sign of them. Not the slightest trace of an Orc's aura. So what have you got to say about that?'

'Maybe he's out of practice . . .'

'Out of practice?' roars the Captain. 'I'm talking about Kemlath Orc Slayer! Back in the war he detected enough Orcs to fill the Stadium Superbius.'

'Really? Kemlath Orc Slayer? I'd no idea he lived down this way.'

'Well, he does. And he's not at all pleased at being hauled out of his villa on a wild Orc chase. Thanks to you the country's in an uproar and I've spent the afternoon up to my knees in mud instead of sitting warm and dry in the barracks.'

He goes on for some time, much of it in language he really should not be using in front of a young female servant of good birth. I'm pretty sure he's about to turn us over to the local Civil Guards just to teach us a lesson but eventually he seems to run out of steam and simply tells us to leave and never come back.

'If we see you round this way again, you'll be sorry.'

'What about our investigation?' protests Makri.

The Captain turns to his Sergeant. 'This is what it's like in Turai these days. Degenerate. They have Orcs dressed in bikinis working as Investigators.'

For a moment I think Makri's about to explode. I quickly pick up the magic dry cloak and toss it at her.

'Fine, Captain. Sorry to bother you. We'll be on our way . . .'

I drag Makri out of the room and outside as quick as I can.

'If you attack eight soldiers it'll only lead to more trouble.'

We find our horses and start back to Turai. The rain is pouring down in torrents. Makri is in such a bad mood about the Captain calling her an Orc that I let her keep the magic dry cloak. Meanwhile I am as wet as a Mermaid's blanket. What a waste of time. As we pass the spot where the Orcs confronted us I halt and sniff the air, trying to pick up any trace of their aura. I certainly have enough of my old sorcerous skill left to detect the aura of Orcs for some time after they've departed.

'Nothing,' I grunt. 'It's gone. Someone has magically cleaned it away.'

A huge flash of lightning rips the sky apart. Another storm. It's a two-hour ride home. A long journey in the pouring rain and all I get for my troubles is a Senator's wife throwing up over me.

'Hello, Thraxas!'

I recognise that voice. A Sorcerer, resplendent in the most luxurious rainbow cloak I've ever seen, steps out from his shelter underneath a tree.

'Never did learn to control the weather!' he booms, in a loud, hearty voice I haven't heard for fifteen years.

'Kemlath!'

'Any good with weather spells?' he asks.

'I'm no good at any spells,' I admit. 'I never took up my studies after the war.'

I introduce Makri. Kemlath, being a powerful Sorcerer, will of course immediately realise that she is one quarter Orc but for once it makes no difference. He's a large, hearty man with a great black beard and mounds of gold and silver jewellery. He's obviously done well for himself since we last met.

'Kemlath and I fought beside each other in the Orc Wars,' I explain to Makri, who's puzzled at the appearance of this large, colourful stranger. He earned the name of Orc Slayer from the fine military power of his spells. He sent many an Orc to an early grave and brought the Orcish war dragons crashing down from the sky. Afterwards he was held high in the city's esteem and became an important man in the Sorcerers Guild. He was a brave man too. He didn't just hide behind his sorcery. When his magic ran out, as every Sorcerer's did eventually during the relentless assault, he picked up a sword and stood with us in the last desperate defence.

'What brings you here?'

I tell him I'm doing a little work for Senator Mursius.

'I didn't know you'd moved down to Ferias.'

'Yes. It suits me well here, on the coast. The weather's milder – apart from this damned rain – and I've built a villa. I grew fed up with the city some years ago. It's not the place it used to be.'

I agree with him there.

'What's this about Orcs?' he asks me.

I tell him the story.

He nods. 'Well, Thraxas, if it was anybody but an old fighting companion I'd say they were lying, or hallucinating, but I know you too well for that. If you say there were Orcs here, that's good enough for me. But I can find no trace of them. And tracking Orcs is a speciality of mine. I'd swear I could tell if an Orc had been here, no matter how much another Sorcerer might have cleaned the area.'

The rain beats down. Kemlath invites us back to his villa. We refuse, albeit reluctantly, as we both have to get back to Turai. He promises to look into the matter more fully, and report to me if he comes up with anything.

'Now you know where I am. Be sure to visit!' he says in parting.

'Not a bad guy for a Sorcerer,' says Makri, as we ride off.

'One of the best,' I agree. 'I always liked him. When

the weather clears up I'll take him up on his invitation. As King's Sorcerer in Ferias he is bound to be rich. Did you see the amount of gold and silver he was wearing?'

It's deep into the night when we arrive back at the city. Our horses are exhausted from plodding through mud. It's past the time when the gates are normally shut but I know the gatekeeper and he lets us in.

'Working late, Thraxas?' he calls down from his vantage point.

'Sure am.'

'Going well?'

'Better than rowing a slave galley.'

Makri, as ever, is impressed at my wide range of acquaintances. Most people south of the river know Thraxas.

It's forbidden to ride in the city at night, but it's so wet and we are so miserable that we risk it. I can't see many Civil Guard patrols out doing their duty on a night like this, with the thunder still rolling overhead and the rain coming down in sheets.

In the Avenging Axe late-night drinking is well under way, fuelled by some raucous singing to the accompaniment of Palax and Kaby, two street musicians who live in a horse-drawn caravan out the back. They spend their days busking and their nights playing and drinking in the tavern. Gurd gives them free drinks for entertaining the customers, which makes me feel somewhat jealous as I grab a beer and he chalks it up on my slate. If I don't make some progress on the Mursius case I'm going to have difficulty paying my bill at the end of the month.

Makri takes a beer and joins me at a table.

'What a waste of time that was.'

She nods in agreement. 'Although I did pick up these,' she says, drawing out some small plants from her bag. They have tiny blue flowers, quite unlike anything I've ever seen before.

'Unusual, I think. I took them from the window box while the soldiers were berating you.'

'Well done. I hope it keeps the Professor happy.'

We wonder what the Orcs were doing in Ferias. Makri asks me if I'm going to report it to the authorities. I shake my head. The city isn't under attack, so I presume it was some private business being carried out by one of the rich citizens of Ferias. Something to do with dwa, probably. A lot of it comes in from the east. I can't see why anyone would want to make life difficult for themselves by involving Orcs, but who knows what goes on behind closed doors in a place like that?

I grab another beer and a few pastries Tanrose has left over from dinner. Palax and Kaby take a break from playing music and join me at my table. They share some of their thazis with me; they always manage to have the best thazis in town. I start to mellow out. Today was a waste of time but at least I'm sitting comfortably with a few beers and some happy drinkers. Usually, when I'm on a case, things get much worse than this.

Makri has changed into her man's tunic. Some sailors shout across, asking where her bikini is. Makri shouts back that she's not working tonight. They look disappointed. She notices that I'm cheerful, despite the arduous day we've had. I tell her I'm always happy when I'm about to win two hundred and forty gurans. She's still sceptical.

'You might lose. It wasn't even the favourite.'

'Troll Mangler is not going to lose. I keep telling you, I know the owner. It's by far the best chariot in that race. It was only six to one because they hadn't heard of it down in Juval. It's the surest thing I've backed in years. If you had any sense you'd go out early tomorrow and back it yourself.'

Makri doesn't seem to approve. That's the trouble with people who are always working. It annoys them when you pick up a little spare money without making an effort.

CHAPTER
FIVE

Next day I sleep late and don't wake until I'm disturbed by noises in my office. I only have two rooms, one for sleeping and the other for working. It's small but it ought to be private. I rise quietly and creep to the connecting door, sword in hand. There's someone in there all right. I burst through, ready to confront intruders.

It's Makri. She appears to be searching under the couch.

'What the hell are you doing under my couch?' I demand, not particularly pleased to have been woken up after last night's drinking session.

Makri leaps to her feet, a furious expression on her face.

'You idiot,' she yells, and then carries on with some harsh abuse. I'm not fully awake and I find this hard to take in.

'What have I done?'

'I lost my money because of you.'

'What money?'

'The money I was collecting for the Association of Gentlewomen!'

Makri insults me some more. I can't understand what she's talking about till I hear the words Troll Mangler mixed in with her tirade.

'Troll Mangler? Are you talking about the race in Juval?'

'Of course I'm talking about the race. You said Troll Mangler couldn't lose! You and your stupid tips!'

'Didn't it win?'

'No it didn't,' cries Makri. 'A wheel fell off at the first corner! And I went out this morning and put all my money on it!'

This is a staggering piece of news. I sink on to the couch, a broken man. 'Are you sure?'

Makri's sure. She's been down at Mox's watching the gamblers who bet on the favourite pick up their winnings, and she's not very pleased about it. I'm stunned by these terrible tidings and struggle to defend myself against Makri's accusations.

'I didn't force you to bet your money on it, did I? This is bad enough for me, without you making it worse. Troll Mangler beaten! I can't believe it. I was depending on that chariot. There's been some dirty sorcery afoot in Juval.'

'The only thing that's afoot is your inability to pick a winner! I never should've listened to you. Now what am I going to do? I'm broke and I need fifty gurans – today!'

Makri's behaviour starts to make sense. I have a fifty-guran piece hidden under my couch. It's my emergency reserve and is meant to be a secret.

'Is that what you were doing under my couch?' I demand.

'Yes.'

'You thought you'd just take it while I was sleeping?'

'Yes.'

'Why?'

'Because it was your fault I lost my money and I need it in a hurry. I promised it to the A.G. today.'

This is such an outrageous statement that I am left practically gasping for breath.

'You promised it to the A.G.? The Association of Gentlewomen? You promised that bunch of harridans fifty gurans of my money?'

'No,' replies Makri. 'Any fifty gurans would do. But I need it today. And they're not a bunch of harridans. You don't mind me borrowing it, do you? You know I'm good for it. It's the least you can do in the circumstances.'

'That fifty gurans is my emergency reserve,' I roar, dragging Makri away from the couch. 'You go anywhere near it and I'll run you through like a dog. You already owe me the forty gurans I lent you to pay for last term's exam fees.'

Makri is now madder than a mad dragon. So am I.

'How dare you rob my office! You think I want to donate the last of my money to that lunatic women's organisation? Are you insane?'

'I only wanted to borrow it,' protests Makri, wiping some dust off her knees.

'Why do you need fifty gurans for the A.G. anyway?'

'It's the money I collected for them. I spent two months raising that cash. You know how hard it is in Twelve Seas. Everyone's poor and the men won't give anything anyway. I had to move heaven, earth and the three moons to raise even that. I've had easier times fighting dragons.'

'Don't tell me about fighting dragons,' I retort. 'I was fighting dragons before you were born.'

I seem to be straying from the point here. I get back to berating the Association of Gentlewomen, which, while not illegal, is not exactly well thought of by a large part of the city, namely the male part.

The King doesn't like it, the True Church fulminates against it from the pulpit and the Senate has condemned it as seditious. It was established to raise the status of women in the city. After a slow start it has gathered an increasing amount of support from the most unlikely quarters. Membership is not made public, but I happen to know that Princess Du-Akai is a supporter, as are various powerful female Sorcerers.

The Sorcerers Guild admits women. Most other guilds do not, which is something the Association intends to put right. Or put wrong, depending on your point of view. The Association has official recognition and admittance into the Revered Federation of Guilds as its first objective, but that's an expensive business, with fees and bribes needed all along the line. Fifty thousand was the figure Makri mentioned, I believe.

'So, can I borrow it?'

'Of course you can't borrow it. If you promised that money to the A.G. you shouldn't have gambled it away. It's unethical.'

'Don't lecture me on ethics, you fraud!' roars Makri.

I start to laugh. I can't help it.

'So. You lost your money on a chariot. Very amusing. Miss Austerity herself gambled it away. The Queen of Sensible Behaviour blows her cash at the races.'

Makri doesn't take this too well. 'It was your fault, you Orc lover! I'd never have backed that chariot if you hadn't said it was a sure thing.'

Makri is livid at me for giving her a bad tip, but she's even angrier at herself for losing the money. She's had to work hard to get the respect of the local businesswomen who support the A.G. and this isn't going to help.

'I've got to take it Minarixa the baker by noon! You have to help!'

I wave this away. 'I'll forgive you for trying to burgle my offices. I'll put it down to the rashness of youth. But let this be a valuable lesson to you. Never blow the last of your money at the races.'

Makri stares at me. I stare back at her.

'I really worked hard collecting that money. And I came and supported you in court. I'll pay you back.'

I shake my head.

'Come on, Thraxas. It's not like you to be as mean as a Pontifex when it comes to money.'

'I need that fifty gurans,' I tell her

'What for?'

'To win back my money at Mox's. Now depart. I need to be alone with the bad news about Troll Mangler.'

There's a knock at my outside door. Makri departs, looking dispirited. I shake my head. Give my last fifty gurans to the Association of Gentlewomen indeed. Big joke.

The knock sounds again, angry and urgent. My door is generally sealed with a locking spell. This is a common minor spell that I can use at will without having to learn it afresh every time, like one of the major spells, but it can be employed by anyone with the slightest knowledge of the mystical arts. While it's reasonably effective against petty theft, it wouldn't keep out someone who was seriously determined. A few months ago Hanama the Assassin came here uninvited and it didn't keep her out for more than a second. I mutter the appropriate incantation, and the door springs open.

It turns out to be Carilis, the not very friendly employee whom we met yesterday in Ferias, looking after Sarija. She has mud all over her fancy black boots and water drips from her elegant blue cloak.

She strides in and looks around with disapproval. 'What a mess.'

'If I knew you were coming I'd have had it cleaned.'

'How can you live in such squalor? It's disgusting.'

I glare at her. I'm starting to feel some disgust myself.

'Did you just come here to lecture me about the state of my office?'

'Doesn't everyone?'

'Some people are too polite. The rest are in too much trouble to care.'

'Well, I find it very offputting. You should do something about it.'

'I will. I'll throw you out on your ear if you don't get down to business. What do you want?'

She stares at me like I'm something that just crawled out from under a rock, but swallows the rest of her criticism and gets down to business.

'Mursius's belongings.'

'What about them?'

'He's hired you to find them?'

'Maybe.'

She leans over the desk and drops a scrap of paper in front of me.

'You'll find them there if you hurry,' she says. She rises swiftly and departs without a backward glance.

I look at the paper. It has an address written on it. One of the old warehouses next to the docks.

I find my magic dry cloak. This case might be even easier than I thought.

The rain has halted and a hot breeze blows in from the sea, raising steam from the streets. The stals, the small black birds that infest the city, risk a few chirrups and venture from their perches high up on the tenement roofs. In the Hot Rainy Season they usually hang around looking miserable like everyone else.

When I'm halfway down Quintessence Street I realise I haven't had any breakfast. I'm hungry. It strikes me that it will soon be time for prayers. I hurry though the mud, keen to get indoors before Sabam, the call for morning prayers which rings out through the city as regularly as clockwork every morning. It's a legal obligation for all citizens to kneel and pray, no matter where they are. Anyone found not complying is charged with impiety, and there's no way round it. Naturally, most citizens take care to be in some suitable place, but if you happen to be in the street at the time, then you have to pray there. Three times a day. It gets me down. It could be worse. Up in Nioj, where things are much more strict, they have six prayer calls a day. Last time I was there on a case my knees ached for a month.

I make it to the harbour and head for the warehouse. Unfortunately, before I reach it, the call rings out from the tower of the nearest church and I am obliged to kneel and pray. I'm seething with frustration. This sort of thing makes it hard to be an Investigator. If anything is going on in that warehouse, the culprit will have plenty of time to cover it up before I arrive.

All around the dock workers are kneeling down so I can't risk ignoring the call. I'd be reported for sure and hauled in front of the special clerical court for impious behaviour. Bishop Gzekius, head of the True Church locally, would relish the chance to send me away for a long trip on a prison galley. He hasn't forgiven me for putting a stop to some nefarious operations he was engaged in earlier this year.

As I'm kneeling, the rain starts again. I pull my cloak tighter around me and wonder how anyone is meant to pray in such circumstances. Finally prayers are over. I hurry towards the warehouse and step inside. The interior is set up with pens and feeding troughs for receiving livestock but the warehouse is empty. I follow my instincts and mount the metal staircase to where the manager's office should be. I find the office, but there's no sign of any manager. No sign of anyone at all.

The door is locked. I bark out the common opening spell and it springs open. I walk in. It's dark apart from a narrow shaft of light coming through the shutters. I wrench them open. Light floods in, and I look around me. The room is full of artwork. Nine or ten sculptures, a few paintings and what looks like a very fine old antique chest inlaid with gold and ivory. I nod. I can't help feeling some satisfaction. When it comes to investigating I'm number one chariot for sure. Hire Thraxas to find your missing works of art, and what happens? He finds your missing works of art the very next day.

It looks like quality goods. There's a small statue of an Elf Maiden which might even be by Xixias, the famed Turanian sculptor who lived in the last century and whose work is now highly prized. I glance at the paintings. High quality again. One catches my eye immediately. It's the painting Mursius was most keen to get back. It depicts a group of young men, one of whom is Mursius. He's in the uniform of a Captain and he's standing with a group of other soldiers, all in dress uniform with swords at their hips and long spears over their shoulders. The inscription on the bottom reads: *Officers of the King's Fourth Regiment* after the successful defence of Turai against the Orc Invaders.

I was there as well, doing my share of defending. No one painted me afterwards.

If I'd prepared for this eventuality I might have been able to load some carrying spell into my mind enabling me to take this lot home with me. But I didn't. Which means I need some form of transport, and quick. I hurry out of the warehouse and look around. The dockers are unloading crates of what looks like Elvish wine from a small vessel tied up in the dock. I approach the foreman, a man I know slightly from drinking in the Avenging Axe. I ask him if I can hire his wagon.

He shakes his head. I take out ten gurans. He shakes his head again. I take out another ten. He tells his men it's time to take a break.

'Have it back in half an hour,' he says, and pockets his twenty gurans. That's quite a sum for hiring a wagon, but I'm sure Senator Mursius won't mind the expense. As I'm leading the horse-drawn vehicle back towards the warehouse I suddenly sense something unusual. Nothing I can name, just unusual. I halt, trying to identify it. Sorcery? I can't tell, it's too faint for my senses. A clap of thunder overhead breaks my concentration but the feeling returns as soon as I re-enter the warehouse and it quickly gets stronger. Everything looks the same but I know that something has happened. This place reeks of sorcery. I draw my sword and tread softly up the stairs.

I pause outside the office door. My senses are going crazy. I take a deep breath and kick the door with all my might then charge in with my sword raised. There's no one inside. The room is empty. And when I say empty I mean empty. Of the sculptures and paintings, there is no sign. Damn.

I swear out loud. In the few minutes I've been outside I've been outsmarted by a Sorcerer. I vent my frustration by kicking a cupboard door. It swings open slowly, propelled by some weight behind it. I watch with horror as a body slumps forward to lie sprawled at my feet. It's Senator Mursius. Blood seeps out of a wound in his back. He's dead.

I stand there staring stupidly at the corpse, trying to work out what's happened. Suddenly heavy boots sound from outside, thundering up the stairs. There's no time to flee and nowhere to hide. A platoon of Civil Guards bursts into the office. As soon as they see me standing beside the body they surround me, swords drawn. Their Captain bends down and examines the body.

'It's Senator Mursius!' he exclaims.

I'm arrested on the spot. Within a minute I'm in the back of a covered Guard wagon on my way to the main Twelve Seas Civil Guard station.

'You're in serious trouble,' mutters one of the Guards.

Senator Mursius was a hero of Turai. It doesn't take a genius to work out that I am the number one suspect for murdering him. I am in trouble. Lightning flashes overhead as I'm led out of the wagon and into a cell.

I was right. My cases usually do turn bad. This one just went very bad indeed.

CHAPTER
SIX

At the Guard station they fling me into an underground cell which is as hot as Orcish hell and stinks like a sewer. The Guards all know me but there's no one likely to do me any favours apart from young Guardsman Jevox, and he's nowhere to be seen. Civil Guards don't like Investigators. In particular, they don't like me. The Guards are under the control of the Prefects in their area. The last Prefect of Twelve Seas, Galwinius, was a man of such corruption that they should have given me a medal for my part in running him out of town, but the Guards don't appreciate a Private Investigator cutting off their supply of bribes. I haven't met Galwinius's replacement Drinius yet, but I doubt he's any better.

A Sergeant questions me for a while. I tell him I had nothing to do with the murder and I'll give him the full story when my lawyer arrives. He tells me that that will probably be a long time.

'Why did you kill the Senator?' he demands.

I shake my head wearily. If he didn't believe my denial the first ten times, I doubt I'm going to convince him now, so I clam up and wait for someone else to arrive. Everyone in a Guard cell is entitled to a Public Defender, but that doesn't mean you'll actually get one. They don't go out of their way to respect your civil liberties in Twelve Seas. I should have my own lawyer on a retainer, but I can't afford it.

It seems obvious that Carilis has set me up for the murder, but I have no idea why. The door opens and in walks Prefect Drinius, his toga edged in yellow to denote his rank. He's a tall, lean man with aquiline features and close-cropped hair, still dark. He can't be much more than a couple of years older than me. I've an idea he fought in the war, which says something for his character. Many city officials managed to avoid it. He has the well-modulated voice of the aristocrat who learned rhetoric at school.

'Did you kill Senator Mursius?'

'No.'

'Explain to me what you were doing there.'

I repeat my request for a lawyer. It's never a good idea to give statements to the Guard without one present. And I'd as soon not have to blacken Mursius's reputation by spilling the truth about his wife. Even though Mursius is dead I still feel some obligation to protect my client's good name.

Drinius informs me that I'll get a lawyer when he's ready to provide me with one. 'I am aware of your reputation, Thraxas. You take pleasure in interfering in the business of the Civil Guards. I do not intend to let you meddle now that I am in command.'

'You ought to be grateful. There wouldn't have been a vacancy if I hadn't exposed Galwinius's corruption.'

Drinius almost smiles. 'Perhaps. I understand the Consul himself was pleased. But as you are no doubt aware, it did not increase your popularity among the Civil Guards.'

'I've never been really popular with the Guards. I try and try but they still don't like me.'

Drinius motions for his scribe to come to his side.

'Put it on record that the prisoner refused to make a statement.'

The scribe puts it on record. Drinius dismisses him and the Sergeant.

'Thraxas, I am not the sort of man to leap to conclusions. You may have a good explanation for what you were doing in that warehouse, but as things stand just now, it looks bad for you. You were found next to Mursius's body. He had been dead for a very short while. The Guard Sorcerer who checked the office found no trace that anyone else had been there. No one at all. Just you and Mursius. Well?'

'Well, he's wrong.'

'I doubt it. Furthermore, our Sorcerer reports that no sorcery was used in the area.'

This surprises me. I wasn't expecting the Prefect to try and trick me with such an obvious untruth. The room reeked of sorcery, which would have lingered for a long time after I'd left. Drinius sees my surprise.

'Are you claiming that sorcery had been used? If so, you're lying. No sorcery was found. Our Sorcerer is quite certain on that point. Which just leaves you and Senator Mursius. And he's dead. Is there anything you'd like to say?'

'Yes. How about some food? I haven't eaten today.'

Drinius shrugs, and departs.

A Guard locks the cell and insults me through the barred slot in the door. 'Things were good when Galwinius was Prefect. Then you stuck your nose in. Now we're going to hang you.'

I don't know what to make of Drinius. I'd assumed he was your standard corrupt Prefect but in reality he doesn't seem so unreasonable. But why bother lying that no sorcery had been used in the warehouse? That wouldn't stand up at the trial. A Guard Sorcerer wouldn't perjure himself about something like that. Even weeks after the event a really good Sorcerer working for my defence could prove that magic had been used at the scene. The Guard Sorcerer would look foolish in court and the Sorcerers Guild would be down on him like a bad spell for abusing his skills. Odd.

The door opens. Breakfast arrives. Bread, cheese and water. All fresh. Perhaps Drinius isn't so bad. Prefect Galwinius would have let me starve.

I wonder who did kill the Senator. Strictly speaking I shouldn't have to worry about it. I only work when I'm paid. The Senator hired me to recover his works of art. I recovered them. Then they went missing again. But now he's dead there's no one to pay me to find them again, which kind of ends my involvement. Unless they do accuse me of the murder, and I end up having to clear my name. I sigh. If that happens, I'll end up investigating with no one to pay me. Private Investigator. What a life.

The door opens. Young Guardsman Jevox appears. I helped him in the past, and he owes me a few favours.

'Thraxas,' he says urgently. 'You're in serious trouble.'

'So they keep telling me.'

'I can't stay here. But I've sent a message to the Avenging Axe.'

He disappears. The day gets hotter and I feel more and more in need of a beer. Sabap, the call for afternoon prayers, rings through the city. I kneel and pray. No sense in giving them something else to get me on. Shortly afterwards the door opens.

'Someone to see you.'

Makri walks in. The door closes behind her.

'In the cells again, Thraxas? They ought to put your name on the door.'

'Very funny. How did you get in here?'

'I said I was your wife. And they believed me, which doesn't say much for your reputation. Or mine, come to that.'

'Well, thanks for coming. I need you to—'

Makri interrupts me. 'Let me guess. The case you were working on has now gone drastically wrong. You have annoyed the hell out of the local Prefect and to make matters worse you are now a prime suspect for murder. You need a lawyer, but they won't bring you a Public Defender so you want me to get you one. Correct?'

'In every detail.'

'Funny how it always happens that way,' says Makri, grinning.

Gurd and Tanrose tell me that Makri has a very attractive smile. I don't really see it myself.

'So, have you seen Gosax?'

Makri sneers.

'Gosax? That cheap crook? He's about as much use as a eunuch in a brothel.'

'Maybe, but he's the only lawyer I can afford.'

Makri looks serious.

'I saw Kerk.'

Kerk is a dwa addict and dealer who, on occasion, passes me information he picks up on his travels.

'He says this time you're really in trouble.'

'So everybody tells me. Why does Kerk say that?'

'Because Senator Mursius is a hero of Turai and the Guards really think you killed him. You've been thrown in jail on trumped-up stuff in the past, Thraxas, but this time they think it's for real. Did you kill him?'

'Of course not! Why would I?'

Makri shrugs. 'Who knows? Maybe someone paid you. After the Troll Mangler debacle you need a stake for the big race meeting.'

'Makri, I liked it better when you'd just arrived in the city and hadn't learned how to make smart comments all the time. I've no idea who killed Mursius but when I was there the place stank of sorcery and now the Guards tell me that their own Sorcerer couldn't detect any traces of magic at all. Which means either they're lying spectacularly, or I'm involved with someone with great sorcerous power. Enough to completely clean up all traces of his actions, which isn't easy.'

Makri's hand keeps straying to her hip. She had to check in her sword at the desk and she doesn't feel comfortable without it.

'You should get a good lawyer,' she says.

'Makri, is there something behind this?'

'Of course not. I'm just concerned for your welfare. I'll get you a good lawyer. By the way, could you lend me some money?'

Makri has not yet developed the art of subtlety.

'Haven't you already removed it from my room?'

'No,' says Makri. 'I was going to, but then I realised Samanatius wouldn't approve.'

Samanatius is a philosopher who sometimes teaches

at the Guild College. He's quite famous. He teaches for free, and gives every appearance of being genuine, unlike some of the charlatans we get round here. Makri likes him. He makes me feel uncomfortable.

'I told Minarixa I'd lent out the money I collected to a woman in distress and I'd have it back in a few days. I promised her sixty gurans.'

'I thought you owed them fifty.'

'Minarixa seemed so disappointed I pretended I'd collected an extra ten.'

Makri pulls a sheet of paper from her tunic. It's a form sheet from Mox's.

'So lend me thirty,' she says. 'And this time pick something good.'

'I only have twenty,' I confess.

'What about your emergency reserve?'

'I'm talking about my emergency reserve.' Sensing that Makri is on the point of lecturing me about drinking my money away, I explain to her about the hefty bribe I had to pay out down at the docks. 'To make things worse, my boots fell apart in the rain. You know how much it costs to get a new pair of boots? Anyway, I can only lend you ten. And I'm not forgetting the forty you already owe me.'

Makri nods. She runs her fingers through her wet, tousled hair.

'Do you know any good lawyers?'

'None that will do me any favours,' I admit.

'How about Cicerius?'

'He's the Deputy Consul.'

'But isn't he a lawyer as well? I'm sure I read some courtroom speeches he made in my law class.'

I explain that while Cicerius is a fine lawyer, he isn't the sort of man you can drag down to Twelve Seas to get you out of the slammer.

'He only works on cases of national importance.'

'Well, I'll see what I can do,' she says.

I study the form sheet for the day's races at Juval. The best bet I can see is Orc Crusher, a good chariot who's won for me in the past. Unfortunately he's a strong favourite and the odds are five to four on. When I explain to Makri that this means if she bets five gurans she'll win only four she's a little disappointed. I tell her there's nothing else really worth gambling on, particularly as we're not in a position to take chances.

'I hope you're right about this one, Thraxas. I'll bet my ten gurans. If I win eight it'll be a start.'

I tell her to put the same bet on for me. Makri bangs on the door, summoning the Guard. He lets her out.

'So what's it like being married to a half Orc?' he asks me when she's gone.

'She's only a quarter,' I reply.

'I reckon you'd be better off being hanged,' he says, and slams the door.

I wait in the cell for hours. No one comes to see me. I feel so starved of company I'd be glad if they interrogated me again, but all that happens is a stony-faced guard brings me more bread, cheese and water. Maybe they're trying to bore me into a confession.

Finally Drinius returns. There's a strange, troubled expression on his aristocratic face. He gazes at me for a few seconds before speaking.

'Your lawyer is here.'

'Good.'

'I was unaware that you were represented by Deputy Consul Cicerius.'

So was I. I can't believe that Makri has managed to bring him here. No wonder Drinius looks troubled. If you're starting out on your political career in Turai you don't want to be caught maltreating a prisoner by the Deputy Consul. Cicerius has little in the way of human warmth, but he's a stickler for the law.

The Prefect departs and Cicerius enters, wearing the green-edged toga that denotes his rank. I notice his sandals are quite dry despite the rain outside. Of course an important man like Cicerius would be ferried here in a wagon and escorted to the door by a servant with a parasol. They might even have laid out a special carpet to protect him from the mud.

'I understand you need a lawyer,' he says, somewhat dryly.

Deputy Consul Cicerius is by far the best orator in the city and has won numerous sensational cases for the defence in the law courts. He's not a crowd-pleaser but he is respected by all for his irreproachable honesty. Although he is a bastion of the Traditional Party and a strong supporter of the Royal Family, he has not hesitated to defend opponents of the King in court if they happen to be innocent. But while everyone trusts Cicerius, he is not exactly well liked. His character is too austere, and he exudes too little warmth to be genuinely loved by the masses. And he is not well born enough to be totally accepted by the aristocracy. He's aware of his brilliance, and his vanity shows. He's a self-made man, respected by all. I wonder if it bothers him that no one much likes him. Possibly.

I thank him for coming, telling him I'm glad I was able to help such an esteemed character as himself with his recent difficulties. He informs me sharply that he did not come out of any sense of obligation.

'You were adequately paid for your services. You should not expect any favours from me, Thraxas. If you do, you will be disappointed.'

I'm disappointed already.

'Then why are you here?'

He tells me he is repaying Makri for a service. I blink. Service from Makri?

'My official wagon became trapped in the mud as we progressed along Royal Way. Some hooligans from the Populares seized the occasion to toss mud and rocks at me. I was in a most uncomfortable position. Your friend Makri fortunately appeared on the scene. She dealt with my tormentors in a most convincing manner.'

This sort of political violence is common in Turai. When it comes round to election times it's swords instead of rocks.

'As a result of which I agreed to her request to help you. In truth, I was not unhappy to do so, because you have featured in my thoughts recently. I believe you may be able to be of service to me. However, that can wait. Firstly, I must get you released from this cell. Tell me the circumstances surrounding your arrest.'

I tell him the full story, omitting nothing.

'In that case they have nothing to hold you on. The case against you is entirely circumstantial. I will arrange your release immediately.'

He leaves the cell. He arranges my release immediately. I am instructed to stay in the city. We leave the Guard station.

'Thank you, Cicerius. What now?'

'Now we have an appointment with Makri at the Avenging Axe. Come.'

He leads me to his official wagon, which takes us slowly through the sodden streets of Twelve Seas.

'She is an interesting woman,' says the Deputy Consul, suddenly.

'Who?'

'Makri. Is that her only name?'

'As far as I know.'

'I had planned to introduce a bill banishing all people with Orc blood from the city. They only cause trouble and are rarely loyal citizens. But I may delay it for a while.'

Somehow this doesn't surprise me. Makri has this odd attribute of making herself popular with the most unlikely people. I used to put it down merely to the sight of her bursting out of her chainmail bikini, but it seems to go further than that. Cicerius has no known track record of being impressed by any young woman's shape, but already he seems to have taken to her.

We pull up at the Avenging Axe. Vendors still grimly try to sell their cheap wares and the prostitutes still ply their trade with any soul brave enough to face the weather. The beggars, having nowhere else to go, still sit in useless misery in the mud, homeless, hopeless, deformed, a sight to raise pity in anyone's breast, anyone apart from the entire population of Twelve Seas, who see it every day.

To my annoyance Kerk chooses this moment to waylay me. Kerk deals dwa but he uses far too much of his own product. He's around thirty, gaunt, with large eyes, possibly displaying a faint trace of Elvish blood, no doubt the result of some distant union of an Elvish visitor and a Twelve Seas whore. Even Elves have to enjoy themselves sometime, I suppose, when they're not sitting in trees singing about stars and rainbows.

Cicerius looks on with disapproval as the bedraggled Kerk plants himself in front of me. I tell him I can't talk now but if he comes across any of Mursius's missing works of art I'll be interested to hear about it. I give him a small coin, which he glances at with disgust before tramping off through the mud and rain.

Makri is waiting for us inside. She looks pleased with herself.

'Thanks for the lawyer. Did you put on the bet?'

She nods. I make a fast trip to the bar. Deputy Consul or not, I haven't eaten properly all day. Bread and cheese are nowhere near enough to satisfy the healthy appetite of a man my size. And I haven't had a beer for more hours than I care to think about. I order a fair selection from Tanrose's dinner menu and a 'Happy Guildsman' jumbo-sized tankard of ale, and then proceed to get them inside me as quickly as I can.

Cicerius is more accustomed to the Senate and the law courts than Twelve Seas and is uncomfortable in the public bar. Everyone is staring at him, wondering what an important man like him is doing here. He insists that we retreat to my office immediately. I nod, but stop off on the way for another 'Happy Guildsman'. You can't expect me to function properly if you starve me of beer. It just can't be done.

CHAPTER
SEVEN

Cicerius's crisp white toga stands out like a beacon in the shabby surroundings of my office.

'To business,' he declares. 'I need the services of a man who has experience of the seamier side of this city, someone who also has a knowledge of chariot racing and all its mechanisms. You qualify for that, I believe.'

'Absolutely.'

'Since our recent encounter, Thraxas, I have looked into your career. I find that though you were a notably bad student as a Sorcerer, and have rarely held down a regular job, you did serve well in the Army. Senator Mursius himself spoke highly of your fighting qualities.

'It is unfortunate,' he continues, fixing me with the sort of stare that can terrify an opponent in court, 'that you could not apply yourself properly in the rest of your life. Your time as Senior Investigator at the Palace was continually marred by periods of drunkenness and insubordination, of which I myself have seen evidence. And where has such behaviour got you?' He gestures round at the squalor of my office. 'Do you not even have a servant to clean for you?'

I can't afford a servant, but I'm not going to admit that to Cicerius. I remain silent.

'Well, it is your affair. If you choose to squander your

talents instead of using them for the good of our nation, no one can prevent you. But I think that you might be of use to me, and I wish to hire you.'

He addresses Makri. 'I believe that you may also be of service. I understand that you speak fluent Orcish, both Common Orcish and the pidgin Orcish spoken in the Wastelands?'

Makri nods. Her eyes narrow at the mention of Orcs.

The Deputy Consul turns back to me. 'You are aware of the Turas Memorial Race, and the entry of a chariot by the Elf Lord Lisith-ar-Moh, who has always been a great friend of Turai?'

'Certainly. I'm looking forward to it. The whole town is.'

'It may surprise you to know that Lord Rezaz Caseg also wishes to enter a chariot in the race.'

I frown. 'Lord Rezaz Caseg? I've never heard of him.'

'You may know him better as Rezaz the Butcher.'

I explode in astonishment. Beer flies everywhere. 'Rezaz the Butcher? *That* Lord Rezaz? But he's an *Orc*, for God's sake! The last time he was in the area he damn near wiped us off the map. What do you mean, he wants to enter a chariot?'

It's one of the most outrageous things I've ever heard. An Orc entering a chariot in the Turas Memorial? And not just any Orc – Rezaz the Butcher! One of the fiercest, most bloodthirsty warlords ever to lay waste to a human settlement. And also, unfortunately for us, one of the cleverest generals ever to destroy a Human army. He was by far the best commander in the Army of King Bhergaz the Fierce, who united all the Orcish lands and led them against us. I pound my fist on the table.

'You don't have to say any more, Deputy Consul. Just tell me what I have to do and I'll do it. I'll prevent that Orc from ever reaching the city. You can depend on me!'

Cicerius looks at me with that steely gaze again. 'That is not what I require you to do. I do not wish you to prevent him reaching the city. Rather I am hiring you to look after the Orcs while they are here. There may be attempts to sabotage their chariot. I need someone to protect against that and see that they are given a fair deal.'

It's not often that I'm speechless. But at Cicerius's words I'm struck dumb. I can't even move my lips. I stand there, staring, wondering which one of us has gone mad. Makri fares no better. She's actually drawn a sword and is looking round her suspiciously as if an Orc might enter right now.

'I see you are surprised,' says Cicerius, breaking the silence.

I'm feeling weak. I fumble for the remains of my beer and try to formulate a reply. Meanwhile I'm straining my mental powers for any sign of sorcery, in case this isn't actually Cicerius but some magical impostor sent to torment me. Finally I utter a few words.

'You can't be serious. Rezaz the Butcher can't really be entering a chariot in the Turas Memorial race. And if he is, you can't expect me to play nursemaid to an Orc! Especially not that Orc. He was leading the assault when the wall caved in. I was there. I lost almost everyone I knew to the Butcher's soldiers.'

'Times change,' replies the Deputy Consul.

'I know. But not that much. Okay, we're at peace just now, but for how long? The Orcish Ambassadors never

appear in public for fear of causing a riot. And this Orc
Lord wants to walk right into the Stadium Superbius and
enter a chariot? Why? And what does the King think
about it?'

'The King is strongly in favour of the idea. You see,
Thraxas, the politics of running a city involves us in
many strange alliances. It so happens that at this
moment it is vital to the interests of Turai that we maintain good relations with Lord Rezaz Caseg. Are you
aware that exploration and prospecting of the various
minerals in the furthest northeast of our territory has
advanced to such an extent that we are about to open
several new copper mines?'

'No.'

'Prospecting has been continuing for some years, and
is now about to pay dividends. You will appreciate the
importance of this to the state. Small as we are in size, we
depend on our wealth for our security. You are of course
aware that there have for some years been border dis-
putes with Nioj?'

Nioj, our northern neighbour, is always finding some
reason to start a border dispute. We already have gold
mines along the boundaries of our two nations and they
would love to get their hands on them. In fact, right
before the last Orc War Nioj invaded Turai. Only the
arrival of the Orcs brought that war to an end as we
Humans were obliged to forget our differences and unite
to face the common enemy.

'Well, once more, the territory is disputed. Although
the deposits of copper are clearly on land that belongs
historically to Turai, Nioj has been making inroads and
may even be about to claim it as hers.'

Cicerius pulls a map from his toga and spreads it on the desk. He points to the mountainous area where the northeastern part of our territory meets the far larger state of Nioj.

'The next territory along is Carsan, populated mainly by nomadic tribes with little state authority. Carsan is in fact under the strong influence of its eastern neighbour Soraz, which sits firmly in the Wastelands between us and the Orcs. And its effective ruler is Lord Rezaz Caseg. To make things as simple as possible, we need support from Carsan to keep hold of the copper mines. And we can't get support from Carsan unless Soraz allows it.'

'So we have to be nice to Lord Rezaz Caseg?'

I look at the map. Soraz looks a long way away.

'Do we really need support from them? What about the League of City-States?' About a hundred years ago all the small states in the region banded together to protect ourselves from large predatory countries like Nioj.

'We can no longer count on much support from that direction.'

I knew that before I asked. The League has been crumbling for a decade, pulled to pieces by the selfishness of its members, including Turai.

'Now do you understand why we wish to accommodate the Orc Lord?'

'Just about. But I don't like it.'

'Your likes are of no concern to the King or the Consul.'

'So I understand. But what's this got to do with chariot racing anyway?'

'Lord Rezaz Caseg is a keen racer, apparently. Furthermore, he has let us know, through diplomatic channels, that he has not forgotten the Elf Lord Lisith-ar-Moh. They fought hand to hand underneath the walls of Turai, but were separated by the press of bodies before a fatal blow could be struck. He tells us that while he respects Lord Lisith-ar-Moh as a soldier he would be pleased to match him in the Stadium.

'The King believes that Rezaz may have other motives. He is under some pressure at home in Soraz from his rival, Prince Kalazar, who is supported by Makeza the Thunderer, a very powerful Orcish Sorcerer. Together they have had some success in gaining support. We believe that Lord Rezaz may be seeking to increase his prestige by defeating the Elvish chariot. Furthermore, with a powerful rival like Prince Kalazar waiting in the wings, he can't allow any instability in the region. If this understanding ensures peace, everyone will benefit.'

I don't believe that we'll ever get any benefit from co-operating with Orcs but Cicerius isn't interested in my opinion.

'The arrival of an Orcish chariot and racing crew will cause some concern in the city,' continues Cicerius. 'It is possible that there may be objections.'

'Objections? There'll be a riot.'

'Let the government deal with riots. You protect against sabotage. If anything goes wrong, you may have the chance to use your investigative powers to put it right. The King is depending on you.'

Cicerius turns to Makri. 'You will appreciate why I also need your help. Very few people in Turai have your grasp of the Orcish language. That, allied with your fighting skills, makes you an ideal person to assist Thraxas in this potentially difficult endeavour.'

Makri has been standing there all this time speechless. She now raises her sword slightly – a terrible breach of etiquette in the presence of the Deputy Consul – and then spits on my floor.

'I'd kill you, the King and all his children before I protected an Orc.'

Well, you can't make it clearer than that.

Cicerius looks puzzled.

'You are particularly averse to Orcs?'

'I am,' explodes Makri. 'I was born in an Orcish slave pit. I lived as a slave till I killed my own Orc Lord and most of his household a year ago. And if you take on the job, Thraxas, I'm leaving.'

'I'm not taking it,' I say, quite emphatically. 'Already people talk about bad luck falling on Turai because we have Orcish Ambassadors here. If more of them appear then every time something goes wrong – from a cup getting broken to a child dying – it will be blamed on them. Senator Lodius's Populares won't have to encourage the population to riot. They'll be out doing it for themselves in no time. Anyone trying to protect the Orcs would soon find their life wasn't worth living. He'd be the most hated man in the city. Protect an Orc? Not me.'

Cicerius leans towards me. 'Yes, Thraxas, you will. The alternative is losing your Investigator's licence.'

'That's not fair!'

'Not fair? I doubt the King would worry himself overmuch about some slight injustice if his wishes were ignored. I myself would not countenance a breach of the law, but consider. You have recently been convicted in court of assaulting an officer of the King. You are at present on bail, suspected of murdering Senator Mursius. It would be entirely right and proper to remove your licence. However, I will stretch a point, provided you do as I request. And you will be well paid.'

'Doesn't it worry you that Orcs are sneaking, treacherous, murderous animals who'd like nothing more than to wipe us off the face of the earth?' I fume.

'Not at this moment,' replies the Deputy Consul. 'We need that copper.'

I ask him when the Orcs are arriving.

'The chariot is coming in by ship in a week or so. Lord Rezaz is already in the city. So is his charioteer. We brought them in discreetly a few days ago. Do not mention this to anyone.'

I won't. The thought that Rezaz the Butcher is actually in Turai at this moment makes me tremble with rage.

Cicerius turns to Makri.

'How is Professor Toarius?'

'What?' says Makri, surprised.

'Your Professor at the Guild College. I understand he dislikes you.'

'How do you know that?'

'He told me when he was my guest for dinner last week.'

Makri shifts uncomfortably, not liking the way this conversation is going.

'He does not approve of women attending the College and would rather you were not there. He can fail you at any time, and fully intends to do so.'

'But I'm a good student!'

'I don't doubt it. Unfortunately the Professor's word will be final. After all, his academic status far outshines that of anyone else at the Guild College. He is seconded there from the Imperial University as a favour to the lower orders by the Consul. If he refuses to pass you then you will not proceed to the next year. If that happens you will never gain the qualifications you require for the University.'

Makri takes a stride back towards Cicerius. She tells him straight out that she doesn't like being blackmailed into doing anything. Cicerius gives the slightest of shrugs, implying that it doesn't matter to him if she likes it or not.

'Are you saying you'll get me into the University if I help?'

'No. The Imperial University does not accept women. Nor anyone with Orcish blood. That is more than I can promise. But I will persuade Professor Toarius to pass you at College, providing your work is acceptable. I understand from other sources that it is indeed of good quality.'

Cicerius stands up to leave. 'Of course, when the time comes, I might be persuaded to use some influence in the matter of the Imperial University. I may well be Consul by then, and I am a very good friend of the Professor in charge of admissions. Who knows how he might react if the Consul were to promise additional funds. Farewell. In the next few days I shall send my assistant with details of what I require from you.'

He leaves the room.

Makri yells in anger and tosses her sword, blade first, into my couch.

'I refuse to protect an Orc!' she shouts.

'And so do I,' I agree.

We light up some thazis to calm us down. I scrabble under the desk for my store of klee, the locally distilled spirit. There are times when beer won't do. The klee burns my throat as it goes down. Makri makes a face, and holds out her glass for more. We sit in silence, letting the day's events sink in. The rain beats on the door and windows. The light fades into evening gloom. After a while Makri breaks the silence.

'So, what are you going to do when they take your licence away?'

'I don't know. What are you going to do when you fail at the College?'

'I don't know.'

We sit in silence a while longer, and smoke some more thazis.

'It's not fair,' says Makri eventually. 'I don't want to protect an Orc.'

'Me neither,' I sigh. 'But it looks like we're stuck with it. Maybe we won't have to do anything. If nothing goes wrong for the Orcs, Cicerius won't need our services.'

'How likely is that?'

'Not likely,' I admit. 'As soon as the chariot arrives the city will be in uproar. The Butcher will be hacked to pieces and we'll get the job of sorting it out.'

Neither of us wants to be involved, but Cicerius has left us no choice.

I pour us some more klee. Makri shudders as she drinks it.

'Why do you buy this firewater?'

'Top-quality klee. It's good for you. You know, I learned long ago to expect strange things to happen. But I never thought I'd end up playing nursemaid to an Orc

Lord at the Turas Memorial. I'm tired. I'd better get some sleep before anything else weird happens.'

A light tap comes on the outside door. It opens. In walks the delicate, dark-clad figure of Hanama. I fumble desperately for my sword. Hanama is number three in the Assassins Guild. The last time I saw her she tossed a dart into the Chief Abbot of a temple of warrior monks, sending him off to paradise rather more quickly than he had anticipated. I make ready to defend myself.

'Relax, Investigator,' she says, in her soft voice. 'Had I been here on business, I would not have knocked.'

I glare at her, sword now firmly in hand. 'Then what do you want?'

'I've come to visit Makri.'

'Just a social call?'

'That is correct.'

Hanama looks at Makri. Makri looks puzzled but gets to her feet and they go off to Makri's room. Strange. I've never known Assassins to do much in the way of socialising.

The door crashes open in the most violent manner. I whirl to face this new intruder. It's Sarija, wife of the late Senator Mursius. She trips and falls. She's wet through. Her face is drawn, with a yellowish hue. And she reeks of dwa, easily discernible even among the multitudinous unpleasant odours that waft in from the street outside.

'I'm hiring you to find out who killed my husband,' she says, then passes out in my arms. I dump her on the couch. I walk over to the door, close it, mutter my locking spell, then barricade it with a chair.

'I don't care who it is,' I grunt. 'No one else is getting in here tonight.'

I notice there's an envelope pushed under the door. When did that arrive? I tear it open and read the message.

You'll be dead before the end of the rainy season, says the message.

'I will be if things go on like this,' I mutter, and throw it in the bin.

CHAPTER EIGHT

The Deputy Consul is blackmailing me into protecting a hated Orcish enemy. A murderous Assassin has just called in to visit Makri. The dwa-addicted wife of Senator Mursius has collapsed in my office after asking me to find out who killed her husband, although I am in fact the main suspect. And now there's another death threat. I hurry downstairs for a beer.

The bar is crowded with thirsty dockers relaxing after their day's work. I squeeze past some mercenaries singing a raucous drinking song and work my way to the bar.

Gurd and I have known each other a long time. As soon as he sees me he can tell I'm troubled.

'You're looking as miserable as a Niojan whore. Guards still after you for Senator Mursius?'

'Much worse,' I reply, and lean over to whisper in his ear. His eyes widen when I tell him about Cicerius and he lets out a Barbarian oath.

'You better get ready to move to another city. Are there any where you aren't wanted by the law?'

'A couple. Nowhere good though. That Deputy Consul is as cold as an Orc's heart. How dare he blackmail me like this?'

Tanrose is stirring a cauldron of soup. I ask her if she

can come upstairs and take a look at Sarija. As well as being an excellent cook, Tanrose is handy with a herbal potion and is competent at dealing with life's little injuries. Since dwa swept the city, she's become competent at dealing with overdoses as well.

We meet Makri and Hanama in the corridor. Hanama is so small, pale and generally childlike it's hard to reconcile her appearance with her reputation. But all the stories are true. People still talk in whispers of the small, anonymous figure who eluded one hundred Simnian soldiers and crawled along the rafters of our Consul's private banqueting hall to fire an arrow into the Simnian Ambassador's heart at the exact moment he undid his impenetrable magic cloak to scratch himself. The Ambassador had plenty of protection with him. I was still at Palace Security at the time and I'd have sworn he couldn't be touched. A great many questions were asked, particularly by the Simnians, but no one was ever tried for the murder. The King swore to the Simnians that he'd track down the killer, but as his own agents had discreetly hired Hanama to do the job, the investigation didn't get very far.

Hanama is distressingly good at killing people. I don't like her at all. I don't like the Assassins, period. Cold-blooded killers, dealing death for money. I've suspected for a while that Makri might be rather closer to the Assassin than she admits and the social call seems to bear it out. It's probably something to do with the Association of Gentlewomen, which I believe Hanama secretly supports. That's Assassins for you, very unpredictable. You can't read their emotions or motives. They're trained not to show them.

Makri bids farewell to Hanama and follows me back into my office where Tanrose turns Sarija on her side to prevent her from choking on her own vomit. I frown. I don't mind too much whether she chokes or not, but I'd rather she didn't do it in my office. It's untidy enough.

My last client, a rich woman by the name of Soolanis, was a hopeless drunk. Now I have a Senator's wife who's a dwa addict. What's the matter with these aristocratic women? They all have nice villas up in Thamlin and plenty of money to spread around. You'd think that would be enough.

Tanrose thinks she'll be fine in the morning, so I dump a blanket on her and leave her on the couch. And then I bid Makri and Tanrose good night, walk into my bedroom, lock the door, put a spell on it, and go to sleep. I've had more than enough for one day. Unfortunately I sleep badly. I'm troubled by dreams of huge Orcish armies rumbling over the Wastelands led by Rezaz the Butcher, on their way to sack Turai.

I wake up sweating, feeling the heat of the city burning around me. I can still hear the screams of my comrades-in-arms as they fell beneath the blades and sorcerous attacks of the Orcs. I was a regular soldier at the time. Gurd was there beside me; he'd joined up as a mercenary. We stood alongside Mursius and a very few others, grimly holding out, seconds from death. A ragged collection of survivors from the regiments had been posted to defend the east wall before it was torn down by the catapults and dragon fire of the invaders. Kemlath Orc Slayer was with us too, I remember. Though young, he'd already gained a great reputation for the military power of his sorcery, and he'd scattered and broken many an Orc battalion with his magic. But by then his sorcery was all used up and he stood alongside us with only a sword for his protection. He was brave, and a good fighter for a Sorcerer.

I remember Captain Rallee, a private like myself in those days, his long golden hair tied back in a braid, picking up a rock to throw as a final act of defiance after his spear was broken and his sword was shattered in the last assault. As the Orcs prepared to overwhelm us, suddenly there was the sound of Elvish trumpets, cutting through the terrible din of battle. Having given up even hoping for it, we were saved by the arrival of Lord Lisith-ar-Moh and the combined Elvish forces from the Southern Islands who'd slipped through the Orc naval blockade in the night and landed just outside the walls of the city.

When the Elves fell upon the rear of the Orc Army it broke and fled. The Elves hunted a great many of them down. Most of us defenders were too badly wounded or too fatigued to join in the chase. All I remember is rescuing a case of klee from a burning tavern and getting so drunk I had to be held upright by Gurd when the Consul came round to congratulate us on our sterling efforts.

Now Rezaz the Butcher and Lisith-ar-Moh are going to race their chariots against each other. Strange times.

I can't get back to sleep. Who killed Mursius? And why? Because of the stolen artwork? They hardly seem sufficient reason. What was he doing in the warehouse anyway? I suppose it's possible he'd somehow tracked down the items himself and had been killed by the thief to prevent him being identified, but I'm not convinced. And what happened to the works of art after that? I know they were removed from the warehouse by sorcery, but it doesn't make sense. Any Sorcerer powerful enough to do that shouldn't need to go around stealing a few statues and paintings. He'd have his own collection.

There aren't that many rogue Sorcerers around, which is fortunate. The Sorcerers Guild regulates its members pretty carefully. There's always Glixius Dragon Killer, I suppose. He seems to operate outside the law when it suits him, although so far he has never been convicted of any crime. I strongly suspect that the death threats are coming from him. It's just the sort of petty malice he'd enjoy. They might be some sort of diversion to distract me from his nefarious schemes. He's wasting his time. I don't have any ideas what his nefarious schemes might be.

I can hear the rain beating down outside. In another couple of days the streets will start to resemble canals and no wheeled vehicle will be able to travel. I get up, light my lantern and go next door. Sarija is still sleeping on the couch. A masked man with a sword is standing over her, about to cut her throat. I wasn't expecting that.

I fling my lamp in his direction. He raises his arm to ward it off and it smashes on the floor. Now there's no light in the room, and I'm facing an armed opponent. Before my eyes have time to adjust I hear him leap at me so I jump sideways, crash into something and fall heavily to the floor.

I'm on my feet in an instant and as my eyes adjust to the gloom I see my assailant trying to outflank me. I let him think I haven't seen him. He thrusts at me with his blade, but I'm ready for it and slide out of the way. I grab his wrist and he grunts in surprise. I drag him towards me.

'You're better than you look, fat man,' he snarls, kicking out at my shin. It hurts but I don't let go till I've pulled him right up to me, then I butt him in the face. He yells in pain as his nose caves in. I like that.

He swings his sword wildly, but he's lost concentration. I stay calm and wait my chance. He makes another rash lunge towards me. I leap nimbly over the still comatose figure of Sarija and he stumbles into her body. I grab a dagger from my desk and fling it at him. It sinks into his chest, and he slumps dead to the floor.

I stare at the body. He wasn't much of a fighter. He should have known better than to attack me. I've had a great deal of experience.

Makri bounds naked into the room with a sword in her hand, alerted by the noise.

'Who is it?'

'I don't know.'

I light a lamp so we can see better. I still don't know. Just some anonymous-looking thug I've never seen before.

'What happened?'

'I found him about to kill Sarija.'

Sarija has not woken up. Powerful stuff, dwa. Maybe it would make me sleep better.

I haul the body out of my room and carry it along the street, where I dump it in an alley. I don't want to report this to the Civil Guards because it'll only give them an excuse to make my life even more difficult. The rain immediately washes out all trace of my footprints, not that the Guards will spend a lot of time looking for clues anyway. If you're found dead in an alley in Twelve Seas it tends to be regarded as the natural order of things. When I return Makri has put a tunic on.

'Couldn't you have done that before you came in the first time?'

'What for?'

'Just one of these civilisation things. Round here young women don't rush naked into men's rooms.'

'You wouldn't be saying that if there had been four of them and you needed me to help.'

'I suppose not. Don't you wear anything when you sleep?'

'No. Do you?'

'Of course. Sleeping naked is only for Barbarians. Like eating with your fingers.'

'What if you're in bed with someone?'

'You still use cutlery.'

Makri says that now she's up she'll use the few hours before dawn to study some philosophy. She attended a public lecture in the forum by Samanatius and she's been puzzling about eternal forms ever since.

'Do you think it's true that somewhere in the universe there is one great, perfect axe of which my own axe is just a pale reflection?'

'No.'

'Samanatius says it's true. And he's the wisest man in the west.'

'Says who?'

'Everyone.'

I start on a joke but bite it back. Makri is keen on her philosophy and can get upset if I mock. As she rushed into my room to save me I figure I might as well be polite for a while. She asks me if I'm going to take on the case for Sarija. I tell her I will, if Sarija ever wakes up.

'I need the money. Anyway, I want to know who killed Senator Mursius. He was my commander. I owe him. What did Hanama want?'

'Some advice on gambling.'

'Gambling? Hanama? What for?'

'It's private,' replies Makri.

'Why would she ask you about gambling?'

'Why not? After all, I'm a woman who just won eight gurans on Orc Crusher.'

The chariot came in an easy winner, winning eight gurans each for Makri and myself.

'So now I have eighteen gurans,' says Makri. 'What's the next bet?'

I see that Makri is not going to tell me any more about Hanama the Assassin, so I let it pass for now. Makri takes tomorrow's form sheet from my desk and spreads it out.

'You're keen on the chariots, all of a sudden.'

'I've no choice. If I don't come up with sixty gurans pretty soon I'll be in disgrace with the Association of Gentlewomen. It's all your fault really.'

I promise to study the form for the next races.

Sarija wakes with the dawn. For a woman rich enough to buy the finest food, cosmetics and hair-dressing skills that Turai has to offer, she's looking pretty rough. I try and get a little breakfast inside her but she has no appetite and barely manages a mouthful of bread. I eat heartily and ask her for some details of the case.

'I'll find the killer. I have to. I'm the main suspect.'

Sarija asks me if I did kill him. I assure her I didn't. She seems to believe me.

'Who do you suspect?'

I admit I have no real suspect. Apart from Sarija, possibly.

'Why me?'

'You can't have been getting on too well together. He won't give you money in case you spend it on dwa. In return you sell off a few works of art and he hires an Investigator to get them back. It doesn't add up to a very harmonious household.'

She admits that what I say is true but points out that she had no reason to kill Mursius.

Not strictly true, I reason. If Mursius wasn't around to interfere, all the family money would revert to the control of Sarija, giving her unlimited access to dwa. Dwa has already proved an ample motive for murder many times in Turai. I ask her where she was when Mursius got killed.

'In Ferias. The servants can testify to that.'

'Servants can generally testify to anything. Did anyone else see you, anyone not connected with the household?'

She shakes her head. It doesn't seem to have occurred to her that she might well be a suspect. 'Surely any Sorcerer could clear me?'

'Maybe. A powerful Sorcerer like Old Hasius the Brilliant at the Abode of Justice can sometimes look back in time and see what happened. But it's a hard thing to do. Depends on the moons being correctly aligned at both the time of the crime and the time of the enquiry. More often than not it's not reliable. That's why we still have people like me to investigate things. Do you know why Carilis came to see me yesterday?'

At the mention of Carilis, Sarija makes a face. 'I've no idea.'

'You didn't like Carilis?'

'She was sent by my husband to make sure I didn't get any dwa. Of course I didn't like her. And I think she had an idea in her head of replacing me.'

'Replacing you? As Mursius's wife?'

Sarija nods. 'That's why I was still able to buy dwa. Carilis was meant to be preventing it, but she'd always turn a blind eye, hoping I'd die from an overdose so that she could move in. She figured it was time she married into some wealth. She comes from a good family, but her father lost all his money in some land scandal. They were cousins of Mursius. He took her in.'

I see. I wondered why an obviously aristocratic young woman like Carilis was working as a nursemaid.

'Have you ever considered giving up dwa?'

'Every day. It's not so easy.'

I talk to her a while more. Now her mind is clearer she's not nearly so unpleasant. In fact, I end up rather liking her, particularly when she tells me about the trouble she had with Mursius's relatives after they married. Sarija comes from a decidedly lower class than the Senator and they didn't like that at all.

'My mother was a dancer from Simnia. I kept up the tradition. I used to work at the Mermaid. It was a rough place in those days.'

'It still is. Roughest place in Twelve Seas. I can see why Mursius's relatives didn't like you. How did you meet?'

'During the Orc Wars. You know how class divisions relaxed for a while when the Orcs were at the gate. Mursius used to come into the tavern with some of his men when they were off duty. We fell in love. After the war was over he came back to Twelve Seas, whisked me off in his carriage and married me. I wasn't expecting it. It was good for a while . . .' She spreads her hands. 'But his family never accepted me.'

I sympathise. I suffered much the same sort of thing with my wife's relatives. You can usually tell the birth of a Turanian from their name. High-class women's names generally end in 'is', like Carilis. No one would mistake Sarija for an aristocrat, even if she acted like one.

'Do you have any beer?'

I give her a bottle.

She drinks it with some relish. 'You know the upper classes only drink wine? I haven't had a beer in years.'

I don't tell her about the man I found trying to cut her throat. Maybe he was just a burglar with a mean streak. I doubt it.

She drinks her beer quickly and asks for another. I'm starting to like her. Any friend of beer is a friend of mine. I hope she didn't kill Mursius. We talk about him a while more. Suddenly she starts to cry. Not hysterical, just a slow, sad kind of weeping.

I hate it when my clients cry, particularly the women. I never know what to do. I try patting her hand. It doesn't help much.

'I'll find the killer,' I tell her.

She seems a little comforted, but it doesn't stop her from crying.

An official messenger arrives from the Senate. I rip open the scroll and eye it warily.

Come immediately to the Stadium Superbius, it reads. It's signed by Cicerius. I suspect it's bad news, but really I'm pleased at an excuse to run away from Sarija's tears.

CHAPTER
NINE

The Stadium Superbius is situated outside the east gate of the city walls. It's huge, the largest arena in any of the League of City-States. The chariot-racing track is the longest you'll find in this part of the world. Samsarina's is longer of course, but Samsarina is way out west of here, and far bigger than Turai.

I travel through the pleasure gardens to the east gate. Usually I'm excited by the journey but as the pleasure gardens are half underwater they're a sorry sight and I'm apprehensive as to why Cicerius has summoned me. I guess I'm about to meet an Orc. Furthermore I am currently as wet as a Mermaid's blanket, because I've left the Avenging Axe without my magic dry cloak. Instead I've used my sorcerous capacity to load the sleep spell into my mind. No matter if Lord Rezaz is here at the invitation of the King. I'm not meeting Orcs without some means of protecting myself.

Prince Frisen-Akan owns a villa right next to the Stadium and it is here that Lord Rezaz is staying. His presence in the city is not yet publicly known. A Guard takes me to Cicerius.

'We have a problem,' says the Deputy Consul.

'Already?'

'I am afraid so. Come with me.'

He leads me through the villa. It's as splendid as you
might expect but I'm in no mood for appreciating fine
furnishings. Before I've prepared myself properly Cicerius has led me into a large reception room. There,
standing in front of the window, is the Orc I last saw at
the foot of the crumbling city walls fifteen years ago.

'Lord Rezaz Caseg,' says Cicerius, and introduces me.

Lord Rezaz is large, even for an Orc, and looks much
the same as I remember him, slightly more gnarled,
though it's hard to tell. Orcs tend to be gnarled anyway.
Despite his rank he wears the standard black tunic of an
Orcish warrior. Over it he has a sumptuous dark red
cloak and he carries a golden mace. With him are two
other Orcs, both rather small for the race. Each has dark
shaggy hair, as is normal, and one wears the black garb
of a warrior. He looks mean. The other is unarmed and
turns out to be Rezaz's charioteer.

I am extremely uncomfortable. I'm in a room with
three Orcs and only Cicerius for Human support. Cicerius
was never much of a fighter, even in his youth. I can't
shake the feeling that, diplomatic mission or not, these
Orcs are going to attack me. I prepare the sleep spell.

'I remember you,' says Lord Rezaz, startling me.

'You remember me?'

'From the walls. You fought that day. I saw you. You
were thinner then.'

I'm even more startled, and a little annoyed. The last
thing I was expecting was for Rezaz the Butcher to comment on my weight.

'I am pleased that the man assigned to aid us is a
warrior,' says the Orc Lord.

Cicerius looks satisfied that I've got off to a good start.

A servant brings us wine. Before coming I had determined to decline all such hospitality. I will not share drinks with an Orc, I told Gurd. 'To hell with it,' I think, and take the wine. No point making life difficult for myself.

'Would someone like to tell me what the problem is?'

'Sabotage,' says the Deputy Consul.

'Already? But the chariot isn't here yet.'

'My charioteer's prayer mat has been stolen,' says Lord Rezaz. 'And without it he cannot ride.'

I stare at them, uncomprehending. 'His prayer mat?'

'It is necessary for an Orcish charioteer to place his prayer mat under his feet before competing. Without it he cannot race. Last night someone stole my charioteer's.'

'Can't you give him another one?'

Apparently not. It seems that an Orc gets his own prayer mat from a priest when he comes of age and losing it is a serious matter. A replacement can only be obtained from an Orcish temple and the nearest Orcish temple is some weeks' ride away. As I know nothing about Orcish religion this is all news to me. I wasn't even sure if they prayed.

I turn to Cicerius. 'Isn't this place guarded?'

'Heavily. But the theft still happened.'

'We foresaw that there may be some difficulties during our stay,' says Lord Rezaz. 'But we did not foresee that the moment we arrived in Turai, under the protection of the King, our religion would be insulted and our persons robbed.'

Cicerius is troubled. He can see the copper mines disappearing from under his nose, and with them his favour with the King.

I ask the Deputy Consul if a Sorcerer is working on the case. He looks uncomfortable and confesses that he's worried about asking for sorcerous help. He's concerned that any Sorcerer asked to find an Orc's prayer mat might tell him to go to hell. The True Church in Turai is permanently suspicious of sorcery and consequently the Sorcerers Guild is always wary of any action that might be seen as impious. He says he'll try and arrange some sorcerous help, but meantime I better start looking.

'Who knew that Lord Rezaz was in Turai?'

'The King and his family. The Consul and myself. That's all, apart from the battalion that brought him in. And they're the most loyal troops the King has.'

Few people are so loyal in Turai that they can't be bought, though I don't say this out loud, not wanting to run us down in front of an Orc. I turn to Rezaz.

'Okay, better fill me in on the details.'

He looks blank.

'It's what Investigators do. Take details. Don't you have Investigators in your country?'

'No,' replies the Orc Lord. 'There is nothing to investigate. In my country, no one would be unwise enough to steal my charioteer's prayer mat.'

I take some details. I take some more wine. It's a fine vintage. Being in a room with three Orcs doesn't seem to spoil it at all. Then I take my leave. As he escorts me to the door, Cicerius lectures me about the importance of this matter. I get the impression Cicerius is never happier than when lecturing me about the importance of something.

Back in Twelve Seas Kerk is waiting at my door,

looking like a man who needs dwa. Even the rain cannot entirely wash its smell from his clothes.

He's brought me a small bronze cup that's just turned up at the premises of one of Twelve Seas' numerous dispensaries of stolen goods. He thinks it might be from Mursius's collection. In truth, Kerk has no idea where it comes from and has simply brought me the first vaguely suitable thing he found in order to raise a little money. For all he knows the cup could have been made yesterday.

I let him know I'm not impressed, but pay him a small amount for his trouble. Later I permit myself a satisfied smile. I remember this cup. It was in the warehouse along with the paintings and sculptures.

'Made in distant Samsarina in the last century, if I'm not mistaken,' I tell Makri. 'It was Mursius's all right. I seem to remember he once bounced it off my head after I fell asleep on duty.'

'Right, Thraxas, you know I'm always interested in your war stories. Have you studied the form yet?'

'Makri, you've made a very quick transition from stern moralist to demon of the race track. Give me a chance.'

'No time,' says Makri. 'I have to hand over that sixty gurans soon. The women are starting to talk.'

I take out the latest form sheet from Mox. It's damp, like everything else in the city now. It costs me and Makri more to take these form sheets away. Paper isn't cheap in Turai. Like *The Renowned and Truthful Chronicle*, it's written out by a scribe and copies are then produced by a Sorcerer, or in Mox's case, a Sorcerer's Apprentice, complete with misspellings.

'Let's see. I don't like anything in the first race. Or the second. Maybe the third . . . Sword of Vengeance, six to four. That's a good chariot.'

'What about Castle of Doom?' says Makri suspiciously. Castle of Doom is the even-money favourite and Makri is now dubious of anything that seems risky.

I shake my head. One of its horses injured a leg last season and I'm not convinced it has fully recovered.

'Sword of Vengeance ran two good seconds last year and they've been out training in the west. I reckon it'll win.'

'Well, I hope so,' grumbles Makri. 'My life was stressful enough already before you started me worrying about chariot racing.'

She hands me her eighteen gurans. 'Are you sure that Stadium Sorcerer in Juval is honest?' she demands.

'I think so. More honest than Astrath Triple Moon was anyway. Incidentally I went up to see Lord Rezaz Caseg today.'

Makri reels in surprise. 'What?'

'Up at the Stadium. He's staying at the Prince's racing villa.'

Makri starts preparing for her inevitable bad mood about Orcs. I brush this aside and tell her about the day's events.

'Good,' she says. 'Maybe they'll go home.'

'Afraid not. They're staying. And I'm helping find the prayer mat. Bit of a weird crime. Not what I was expecting.'

Makri tells me that it was a very smart crime. 'What better way would there be to make sure the Orcs don't enter the race? If someone sabotages the chariot after it arrives, it could always be fixed. I presume the King will place the services of Turai's wagonsmiths at the disposal of Rezaz. Even the horses would be difficult to harm because Cicerius said they're bringing a spare team. But the prayer mat is a clever target. No Orcish charioteer will ride without his mat. If he dies in the race he wouldn't get to heaven. And there's no chance of getting another one to Turai in time, not in this weather. Didn't you know about Orcish charioteers and their prayer mats?'

'No. And neither did anybody else in Turai, apart from whoever stole it. Why didn't you mention it earlier?'

Makri looks annoyed. 'No one asked me. I don't go around giving out lectures about Orcs. It's not my fault if you're all completely ignorant about their culture.'

'Well, it's fortunate you know so much, Makri, because you're helping me find it. Don't start protesting, you know you have to. If the Orcish chariot doesn't run then Rezaz withdraws his protection from the copper mines. Cicerius will be down on us like a bad spell. I'll lose my licence and you'll fail college. First thing I have to know is who in the city wants the Orcs not to run.'

'Wouldn't that be everyone?'

'Yes. That makes things difficult. But there must be someone with a stronger reason than most. And who would have enough knowledge to pull this off? There can't be many people who know enough about Orcish culture to realise that taking the prayer mat would have such an effect.'

Makri stops being angry and gets depressed. All this involvement with Orcs is really upsetting her. She doesn't like to think about her time as a gladiator slave.

'It's okay when I can just kill them. But I can't stand this collaboration.'

I sympathise. I'm not enjoying it either. And there's still the matter of Mursius's murder to be cleared up. More tramping round in the torrential rain asking questions of people who don't want to answer them. Not for the first time, I curse Rittius for plunging me into poverty and making me work.

I'll take the bronze cup up to Astrath Triple Moon. He's a good Sorcerer and may be able to learn something from it. Before I can do that Captain Rallee appears. He's the officer in charge of the small Civil Guard station next to the docks. The Captain and I go back a long way. We were in the same unit in the Army and fought against the Niojans and then the Orcs. Most times we meet now I annoy the hell out of him. He thinks that when I'm investigating criminal activities I should go running to the Guard every time I find out something. I rarely do.

Incidentally, our careers both took a sharp downward turn around the same time. When I was sacked from the job as a Senior Investigator at the Palace the Captain was moved out of his comfy job at the Abode of Justice due to some political manoeuvring by Rittius, who was then still Deputy Consul. The Captain ended up pounding the beat and he doesn't like it at all. The small station next to the harbour is not the most comfortable place for a man to spend his time, and certainly not a suitable reward for a man who fought bravely for his city. But in the corrupt city that Turai has now become, advancement comes to those with good connections, not to those who have served her well. This, plus the fact that Turai is currently struggling under a dwa-fuelled crime wave, puts the

Captain in a more or less permanent bad mood.

I'm generally pleased enough to see my old fighting companion though a visit from him usually means trouble.

'You're in trouble,' says Captain Rallee.

'Trouble is my middle name,' I reply.

It doesn't raise a smile. 'The name Lisox mean anything to you?'

I shake my head.

'Small-time thug. We just found him dead in an alley, not far from here. He had a knife wound in his chest. Thrown, not stabbed, according to my medical expert. Not many men can throw a knife that accurately, Thraxas. Specialised art.' He eyes me.

'Lots of men learn how to do it in the Army,' I point out.

'Not many as well as you.'

'I expect it was the Brotherhood. They have a lock on crime in the area. You know how they hate any independent men trying to muscle in.'

'You care to hand over your knife for sorcerous examination?'

'I would. But I haven't seen my knife for some time. I lost it on a case and never got round to replacing it.'

'Then perhaps we better just get a Guard Sorcerer down from the Abode of Justice and have him check the aura on the body. See if it has any connection with your office, perhaps.'

'Come on, Captain. The Abode of Justice isn't going to send down a high-class Sorcerer just to check on some vagabond found dead in Twelve Seas.'

'Probably not,' agrees Captain Rallee, realistically. 'So why don't you just tell me what it was about?'

I remain silent.

'What's the idea of reporting Orcs in Ferias?' he demands, taking me by surprise.

'I met some. You don't expect me to ignore them, do you?'

'Well, no one else met them. I hear that Kemlath Orc Slayer himself was down there. If he says there were no Orcs around it means there were no Orcs around.'

The Captain looks thoughtful. I know he's reliving memories similar to mine, of when we knew the young Kemlath and how he fought at the walls.

'Except, Captain, you know I wouldn't make up a story like that. I don't know why Kemlath couldn't find any trace. Someone must have cleaned up the area with sorcery. It was good seeing old Kemlath again. You remember that day when he brought down a war dragon and Gurd was furious because it crushed his tent?'

'Never mind the war stories. What were you doing out in Ferias?'

'Working for Senator Mursius. Not that Ferias falls within your jurisdiction.'

'The Senator was murdered at the docks. That does. Prefect Drinius thinks you killed him.'

'Well what do Prefects know about anything?'

'Drinius is much smarter than Galwinius was. How come you suddenly have the Deputy Consul on your side?'

'Cicerius is always willing to come to the assistance of an honest citizen.'

'So why's he helping you then?'

I decline to answer. I offer the Captain a beer but he doesn't accept it.

He's around the same age as me but much better preserved; tall, strong, broad-shouldered. His hair hangs down his back in a long pony tail. So does mine, but mine is brown, fast going grey, and the Captain's is still golden. A ladies' man, or used to be before he grew too tired of trying to keep the lid on the spiralling crime wave to do anything except work and sleep.

'Last time the Guards met Lisox he was working for Glixius Dragon Killer. Remember him? So maybe you're running into trouble, Thraxas. Now, do you want to tell me about it?'

'There's nothing to tell.'

'Then if Glixius starts getting on your tail don't come running to us for help. And if I find you stepping out of line on this one I'll be down on you like a bad spell. I've enough problems without you adding to my grief.'

He slings his heavy rainproof cape over his shoulders.

'I hate the Hot Rainy Season. It's pouring down out there and I'm still sweating like a pig. If I have to wade through Quintessence Street to visit you again I'm not going to be pleased.'

Weather shouldn't be like this. Thirteenth day of the Hot Rainy Season. Seventeen more to go. Makri was right. It was a dumb place to build a city.

I ponder his news. Glixius Dragon Killer. He's a powerful Sorcerer. Not up to the standards of the greats, but a lot more powerful than me. It seems likely he's behind the death threats. And now one of his thugs is creeping into my rooms, disturbing the occupants. Glixius is a known criminal associate of the Society of Friends. He's never been convicted of anything. Too smart, too many connections. I eat some breakfast, and wonder what it's all about.

I've had a few strange experiences recently. There were the Orcs in Ferias. Then Carilis leads me to the warehouse and Mursius turns up dead. I found the lost works of art and straight away they went missing again. Surely sorcery must have been involved there, though the Guard found no trace of it. And now I'm getting death threats. I finger my spell protection necklace. It's made from Red Elvish Cloth, which forms a barrier against magic. I have a strong feeling that Glixius Dragon Killer is behind this. If he is, I'm going to nail him.

I wonder what Hanama wants with Makri. No time to think about that, not with this business of the prayer mat. Where do I start on that one? Practically the whole city would be willing to sabotage the Orcs. But no one was meant to know they were here yet. Finding out who had advance information seems like the thing to do.

I try the kuriya pool, without success. Kuriya, a dark liquid from the furthest west, is a mysterious substance in which a skilled practitioner can sometimes see events that happened in the past. It's fabulously expensive and I thought long and hard before replenishing my supply recently. It turns out to be a waste anyway, because I draw a complete blank. Maybe there's nothing to see, or maybe with so much going on I just can't work myself into the required trance. Whatever the reason, when I sit down, concentrate the best I can and stare into a saucer full of the liquid, all I see is a saucer full of liquid.

You can't use the same kuriya twice. I pour it out and curse the expense. I ditch the sleep spell from my mind, use my sorcerous capacity to renew my magic dry cloak, and hit the streets.

The rain pours down. First thing I want to do is locate Carilis and find out how she knew Mursius's goods were at the warehouse. After that I'll pay a visit to Astrath Triple Moon and show him the bronze cup.

A young lad at the next corner is selling *The Renowned and Truthful Chronicle of All the World's Events*. As ever, it is written hastily by a scribe and then turned into thousands of copies by their Sorcerer. It purports to cover all important events in the city but in reality it concentrates mainly on scandalous matters, detailed accounts of clandestine meetings between Senators' sons and notorious actresses and such like. I notice that the vendor is looking as happy as an Elf in a tree as he sets out his papers in his stall.

He tilts back his head and lets out a cry. 'Orcs coming to Turai! Orcish chariot due to race in the Turas Memorial!'

Rarely can a newsboy's cry have had such a dramatic effect. Even when the *Chronicle* mistakenly announced that Prince Frisen-Akan was dead from a dwa overdose I didn't see people running through the rain to get their hands on a copy. No wonder the vendor is happy.

When word starts to spread that Rezaz the Butcher is really entering an Orcish chariot in the race there's immediate uproar. Ignoring the rain, people pour out of their homes and workplaces to vent their anger. Soon an angry mob is gathering and voices are raised in furious protest. Among the crowd are the usual collection of troublemakers and criminals but alongside them are many honest citizens, outraged by the shocking news.

With the single exception of the Ambassadors secreted away in the grounds of the Imperial Palace, no Orc has ever entered Turai.

'Death to the Orcs!'

'Kill them!'

'No Orcs in Turai!'

'The city will be cursed!'

The most obvious representative of the King in Twelve Seas is Prefect Drinius. His house is close to the Civil Guard station down Tranquillity Lane and people start marching in that direction. I presume this news has leaked out without the knowledge of the authorities because the Guards seem unprepared for trouble and are slow to react.

The poor of Turai are not averse to rioting but it's not easy to get one going in the downpour. When the Civil Guards finally realise the extent of the problem and start flooding into the area at least there are no burning buildings to hinder them.

I'm as interested in a good riot as the next man but I probably should get on with my investigation. If the Guards seal off the area I'll be stuck in Twelve Seas, and I have to make my way to the rich part of town if I want to find Carilis. I start muscling my way through the crowd. My weight gives me a decided advantage and I barge through the mob. I'm used to this sort of thing. Only this summer there was a massive citywide riot after Horm the Dead, a particularly malignant Half-Orc Sorcerer, unleashed his Eight-Mile Terror Spell on the city. Even now the damage has not been fully repaired. The workmen will be back at their tasks after the rain stops.

What troubles me is the thought that if the Consul's

plans to allow an Orc chariot to race in Turai have leaked out already, then my part in the affair might become public knowledge sooner than expected. It's going to make looking for this prayer mat much harder. I'd better ask Astrath Triple Moon if he can help me with a decent spell for protecting the Avenging Axe from being burned to the ground by an angry mob.

Bricks start to fly. The crowd is turning nastier and the noise of their anger is loud enough to wake Old King Kiben. Finally I make it through Quintessence Street and turn right up Moon and Stars Boulevard. This takes me into Pashish, which, though poor, is generally a quieter part of town. But even here angry crowds are on the streets and squadrons of Civil Guards are out with their shields, spears extending from the front of their ranks to keep back the mob. Kalius the Consul is the subject of vociferous criticism for allowing such a thing to happen. Some voices even berate the King which makes me wonder about the wisdom of this whole policy. I suppose he needs the copper, but this can only bring more support to the Populares, who want to get rid of the monarchy. I find myself next to Derlex, the young Pontifex in charge of the local church. He's not rioting, being a Pontifex, but he's certainly outraged by the news.

'A shameful thing!' he thunders.

'Absolutely.' I agree. 'Orcs in the city – disgraceful. I imagine the True Church will not be pleased?'

'Of course not! We will drive them out.'

'And yet,' I add, 'who knows? Might they pray to the same God as us?'

The Pontifex gasps with horror at this terrible blasphemy. He screams at me that Orcs don't pray to any God that he knows of.

I apologise for my stupidity. The Pontifex moves away. Now there's a man who obviously knows nothing about Orc prayer mats.

I struggle on. When I reach the business and market districts the violence fades away, but even here the atmosphere is tense and angry. The news has spread all over the city and the rich merchants don't like it any better than the poor workers. Everyone hates Orcs here.

The heat that has been building up over the past few days now erupts into an enormous thunderstorm. The sky explodes in flash after flash of lightning and the thunder booms over the city. The rain comes down in such sheets that it's impossible to see where I'm going and I'm driven into a doorway for shelter.

I find myself next to a well-dressed man, a lawyer from the cut of his cloak and tunic.

'We're cursed,' he says, shaking his head, as the storm rages above us. 'You can't invite Orcs into the city and expect nothing bad to happen.'

'Perhaps the King has good reasons for it?' I venture.

The lawyer looks at me furiously. 'Orc lover,' he spits, and strides out into the rain, preferring the torrential downpour to the company of a man who doesn't mind a few Orcs coming for a visit.

I stare out gloomily at the rain. I can see these next few weeks are going to be tough.

CHAPTER
TEN

Carilis is back at Mursius's villa up in Thamlin, close to the Palace. I used to live around here. My old house is occupied by a Palace Sorcerer now. He's a dwa addict, but he keeps it quiet. He makes a healthy living from drawing up horoscopes for ambitious courtiers. Many of Turai's Sorcerers are independently wealthy. Those that have to work earn their money from generally useless tasks, pandering to the rich. Comparatively few do any good for the city, other than Old Hasius the Brilliant, chief Investigating Sorcerer at the Abode of Justice, or Melus the Fair, resident Sorcerer at the Stadium Superbius.

The servants show me in. Carilis laughs when she sees me.

'What's funny?'

'You. You're so fat and your feet are wet.'

'Maybe you can help me with some things I don't already know.'

'Like what?'

No servant has come to offer me wine, or even take my cloak. I dump it on a chair. It's still dry. Good spell.

'Like who killed Mursius?'

'I understand you're a prime suspect.'

'Only in the eyes of the law. So who really did it?'

Carilis doesn't know and she says she's too upset to talk about it. Whether that's because she's lost her lover or her meal ticket, I can't tell.

'How did you know Mursius's artwork was at the warehouse?'

She won't say.

'Were you having an affair with Senator Mursius?' I demand, just to shake her up a bit.

'No,' she replies, and doesn't look shaken.

'Sarija thinks you were.'

'What would that dwa-riddled fool know about anything?'

'That's no way to talk about your employer.'

'Sarija didn't employ me. Mursius did. And I didn't enjoy having to look after his wife.'

I bet she didn't. No young aristocratic woman would enjoy being reduced to the role of servant. That's a terrible loss of status, and status is very important to these people.

'If you want to find out who killed Mursius you'd be better off coming clean. The Guards won't find out anything.'

'I somehow can't imagine that you will either, fat man.'

For an elegant young lady she has very bad manners. I tell her I'm suspicious she set me up for the murder. This infuriates her.

'Are you saying I was involved? I was trying to help Mursius. If you'd done your job he'd still be alive.'

She turns on her heel and walks out of the room. The interview is over. On the way out I pick up a peach from a bowl of fruit and cram it in my mouth. No sense in letting the visit be a complete waste of time. I haven't learned much apart from the fact that Carilis is still living at Mursius's house though, with her employer dead, it surely won't be long before Sarija slings her out.

The thunderstorm has abated, but the rain hasn't let up. Here in Thamlin the effect isn't so bad. Most of the water flows off the tiled roads and pavements into the sewers. The houses round here won't be collapsing when the ground gives way beneath them, as happens every year in Twelve Seas.

My cloak is still dry but my shoes are wet through. I start to wince as the incessant rain pounds into my face. The cloying heat sends torrents of sweat running down my back. A wagon rumbles up, its wheels making a dull noise on the tiled road. Prefect Drinius emerges, followed by three Civil Guards.

'You're under arrest,' he says.

'Fine,' I reply. 'I was getting tired of the rain anyway. What's the charge?'

'Murder. We found the knife that killed Senator Mursius. And guess whose aura is all over the handle?'

'Archbishop Xerius's?'

'Wrong. It's yours.'

The Guards throw me in the back of the carriage.

'Watch him closely. If he tries uttering a spell use your swords.'

Little do they know I'm using my entire magical capacity to keep dry. The Guards keep a careful eye on me as we ride west through Thamlin. The ground rises slowly, sloping up through the wooded area that leads to the Palace. The Abode of Justice, headquarters of the Civil Guards, is located just outside the Palace grounds.

I can make no sense of this development, so I don't try to. I'm an important man in the city, at least for a few weeks. The Deputy Consul needs me to look after the Orcs. He'll get me off from whatever phoney charge Drinius and Rittius have cooked up this time.

The Abode of Justice is a large building, fairly splendid I suppose, though you can't see it in this rain. I used to know everyone here when I was Senior Investigator at the Palace, although Palace Security and the Civil Guards are rivals, and generally fail to co-operate on anything. It takes us a few minutes to enter. The Sorcerer who checks us in takes an age to utter the spells to open the doors and close them behind us. With the unrest in the city, they've stepped up security.

I often get thrown in the cells but twice in two days is excessive. I'll never get anything done at this rate. Damn that Rittius, he's really out to get me. It strikes me how much I want a beer, and how long it will be before I can get one. Once they put you in a cell, they never hurry to question you, the theory being that if they give you some time to worry about things you'll be easier to break. Sound theory for most people, maybe, but I've been in far too many cells to let it bother me. And I get a good break because there's someone in my cell already who turns out to be a big racing fan. When he informs me that Sword of Vengeance cruised home an easy winner I'm so pleased I almost forget I'm incarcerated. I matched Makri's eighteen-guran bet at six to four which means we both won twenty-seven gurans. Makri is edging closer to the sixty she needs. Another couple of wins and she'll be off my back. What's more, I'll have a reasonable stake for the Turas Memorial.

I'm soon deep in conversation about the upcoming
race meeting with my cellmate, Drasius. He's a banker by
trade, who's been having a little difficulty persuading his
customers that his accounts are entirely honest. He's
just heard the news of the Orcish chariot coming to
town and he's of the opinion that it might give the Elves
a good run for their money.

For the first time it strikes me that there is actually an
interesting sporting contest coming up. I've been so
appalled at my unwilling role in it that I haven't considered this before. Moonlit River will certainly be a superb
four-horse chariot. Lord Lisith-ar-Moh wouldn't send it
up from the Southern Islands if it wasn't. I've seen many
Elvish chariots and I've rarely seen one that couldn't
cruise past anything we Humans had to offer. It's said
that the Elvish horsemen can talk to the horses, which
gives them an advantage. There again, what about the
Orcish team? I hadn't given them any chance, but Drasius
the banker points out that Lord Rezaz Caseg wouldn't
send his chariot if it didn't have a chance of winning.

'Why would he? The Orc wants revenge on the Elf
Lord. He wouldn't enter something that was guaranteed
to lose. I figure it's worth making a sizeable investment
with the bookmakers on the Orcs.'

I can see why Drasius might be in trouble with his
customers at the bank. But what he says makes sense. So
far the only reaction I've encountered to the affair has
been the outright hostility to Orcs shown by the rioting
citizens. I'm a little surprised to find someone who's
more interested in the sporting aspect. It starts to make
me feel interested too. Okay, the Orcs are hated enemies
and the only good Orc is a dead Orc, but from another

point of view, a chariot race is a chariot race and I love chariot races more than a Senator loves a bribe.

'They'll be giving good odds on the Orcs,' adds Drasius. 'Even if the bookies rate it, it's not going to get many backers in Turai. The Elves will be strong favourites. The bookies might even push the price out on the Orcs to attract a little money.'

This is true. The Orcs are going to be unpopular, so their price is bound to be high. Bookmakers set their odds partly by the chance they give the chariot of winning, but the amount of support for a chariot comes into it as well. A popular charioteer can attract a load of bets, even if he's not actually riding the best chariot, and when this happens the bookies have to cut the odds just in case he happens to win. Conversely, a good chariot with a chance of winning but which no one wanted to bet on would stay at higher odds. That's an unlikely occurrence normally – why would a chariot with a chance of winning not be popular? But the Orcs might be a special case. Even if their chariot could win, I can't see it being heavily backed by Orc-hating Turanians. There might be an opportunity here. To put it bluntly, it might be a good idea to bet on the Orcs. I hate Orcs as much as anybody else, but one has to be realistic about these things. It certainly offers me an incentive to find their prayer mat.

'I expect Senator Mursius's chariot will have some support for sentimental reasons but only a fool would back it against the Elves,' says Drasius

I didn't realise that Mursius's chariot was still in the race.

'Didn't you hear? His wife's taken over the stable.'

That's interesting. You have to admire Sarija for this. Mursius's chariot is by far the best in Turai. The public would be disappointed not to see it run.

'At least the race will be fair now,' says Drasius.

'How do you mean?'

'I heard a rumour that the Society of Friends was planning some sort of betting coup but I doubt they'll try it now with the Orcish chariot coming. Too much attention.'

'I don't see how they could've planned anything anyway, ' I object.

Betting coups, horse doping and various other examples of nefarious behaviour designed to cheat honest punters like myself are not unknown in the out-of-town meetings, but you can't do that sort of thing at the Stadium Superbius. It's too carefully regulated. Melus the Fair, bless her name, is Stadium Sorcerer and she makes sure everything is above board. Powerful, clever and incorruptible, Melus is the only person in the whole city apart from Cicerius that everyone trusts. Since she took over the job from Astrath Triple Moon, there hasn't been a breath of scandal at the Stadium.

Drasius agrees.

'It's certainly been better. I lost a bundle while that crook Astrath was meant to be keeping things in order. Damn him.'

Astrath Triple Moon was accused of letting sorcerous involvement in the races go unreported after he was heavily bribed to do so. I helped with his defence. I didn't exactly prove him innocent – it would have been difficult as he was guilty as hell – but I muddied the evidence enough for him to be able to resign without prosecution.

I was as outraged as the next man at the idea of cheating at the Stadium, but Astrath was a friend. And he paid me a bundle. I don't mention any of this to Drasius.

'All the races have been fair since Melus took over. But that's what I heard anyway, the Society was planning something.'

The Society of Friends control the north of the city. It's not impossible they'd make some attempt at cheating, though I really can't see how they could pull the wool over the eyes of Melus the Fair.

When a guard comes along and takes Drasius away, I'm sorry to see him go.

'Delighted to share a cell with you,' I tell him. 'Remember my name. If you need any help, just call on me.'

Not long afterwards I'm taken to see Praetor Samilius. For a small state Turai has far too much officialdom. We're ruled by the King but beneath him are a whole host of elected officials, all of them jostling for power. Next in line to the King is the Consul, followed by the Deputy Consul, and then there are the four Praetors, one of whom, Praetor Samilius, is head of the Civil Guard and based at the Abode of Justice. Then you've got the ten Prefects, and a whole Senate to advise them all, and various powerful pressure groups like the Honourable Association of Merchants and the Revered Federation of Guilds and the True Church, not to mention the Army, the Civil Guard and Palace Security.

It didn't used to be like this. Fifty years ago there was the King, a few officials and a whole host of loyal citizens ready to fight for Turai. We were poor, but strong. Now we're rich and weak. It's only a matter of time before Nioj wipes us off the face of the earth.

Praetor Samilius isn't too corrupt by our standards, but he's a harsh man with little feeling of sympathy towards the struggling masses. He is a renowned snob. Like many of our upper classes, he has adopted some rather decadent foreign manners, though he did fight in the war, so he's not soft, despite the vastness of his belly and the rolls of fat around his neck.

'Don't you people in Twelve Seas ever get your hair cut?' he says by way of an opening insult.

'We're wearing it long this season.'

The Praetor's hair is short, grey, and beautifully conditioned. His nails are perfectly manicured, and he smells of perfume. He looks at me with distaste.

'We really should have them washed before we bring them into this office,' he says to his secretary.

He takes a sheet of paper from his desk and tosses it down in front of me.

'What's that?'

'Your confession. Sign it.'

This gives me my first good laugh of the day.

'What am I meant to confess to?'

The Praetor's eyes narrow. 'You know.'

I remain silent. Samilius adjusts his bulk in his chair. He takes a bite from a peach and drops the rest in a wastebasket.

'Thraxas, I can't be bothered getting tough with you. There's no point. Your aura was on the knife that killed Senator Mursius.'

'Says who?'

'Old Hasius the Brilliant.'

I'm shaken by this, though I don't let it show. Old Hasius the Brilliant, chief Investigating Sorcerer of the

Civil Guard, never makes mistakes and is almost impossible to fool. What's worse, he's honest. I remain silent.

'Nothing to say? Not going to ask for a lawyer? Maybe
you expect the Deputy Consul to come to your aid?' He
chuckles. 'He's not going to get involved. Very bad for his
reputation. You're on your way to the gallows. Even
Cicerius and his famous oratory couldn't help you in
court. Not for this. Not when you were found at the scene
and Hasius places your aura on the knife. Why don't you
make our lives simple and sign the confession?'

I remain silent.

'Very well,' says the Praetor.

He makes a big show of signing some official documents, then informs me that I am being arraigned for the
murder of Senator Mursius. I will be held in custody
until I appear in court, where the charges will be laid
against me. The Guards lead me back to my cell. I'm not
feeling too happy with the way things are going. I was
depending on Cicerius to get me out of this, but Samilius
is right. No matter how much the Deputy Consul wants
my help he's not going to come to my rescue if it's certain
I killed Mursius. It would be too damaging politically.

I can't understand it. Hasius says my aura was on the
knife. How can that be? A really good Sorcerer can fake
an aura, just about, but it's difficult, and it would be
almost impossible to fool Hasius. He might be a hundred
years old, but he's still sharp as an Elf's ear on such
matters. If someone stole a knife from me and used it on
Mursius my aura would be on it, but so would theirs.
Hasius only found my aura. It's looking worse with each
passing second. A jury will convict me on this evidence.
If I was in the jury, I'd convict me.

The call for prayers rings out through the Abode of Justice. I get down on my knees and pray. It seems like the smart thing to do. As I finish the door opens.

'Deputy Consul Cicerius and Government Sorcerer Kemlath Orc Slayer to visit Thraxas,' barks the Guard, who sticks his chest out as he stands to attention.

I leap to my feet. 'Kemlath! Am I pleased to see you. And you, Deputy Consul.'

Cicerius looks at me very severely. 'Are you incapable of staying out of prison for more than one day? I would not be here had I not been persuaded to come by Kemlath. How strong is the evidence against you?'

'Strong,' I admit. 'I was there when Mursius was killed and now Old Hasius the Brilliant says my aura was on the murder weapon.'

'And what do you have to say in your defence?'

'I didn't do it.'

'Is that all?'

'What else can I say?'

'That depends on how keen you are to avoid the gallows. This is most inconvenient, Thraxas. I need you to find that prayer mat.'

'And there's nothing I'm looking forward to doing more. But what can I do if Rittius and his gang are out to get me?'

'Are you saying Rittius has manufactured the evidence?'

'Someone has.'

'I'm sure of it,' agrees Kemlath Orc Slayer. 'That's why I persuaded Cicerius to come. An old soldier like Thraxas wouldn't murder his ex-commander. Who knows what may have happened to the evidence?'

Cicerius is looking very dubious. As Deputy Consul he really can't be seen to be continually pulling strings to release a man from prison if that man then turns out to have murdered a Turanian war hero. It would be political suicide. On the other hand, he's relying on me to find the Orc charioteer's prayer mat.

'In view of Kemlath Orc Slayer's opinion that the evidence against you may have been manufactured, I am willing to once more use my influence on your behalf. I shall instruct Praetor Samilius to release you.'

I thank him profusely. He waves it away. 'Just try and stay out of trouble this time.'

He turns to Kemlath. 'Kindly report your findings to me as soon as possible. It is vital that you come up with something quickly. With the evidence being so strong, I will be unable to keep Thraxas out of prison for long.'

P raetor Samilius is about as angry as a Troll with a
   toothache.

'If you try to flee the city I'll have you hacked down at
the gates.'

Murder trials are traditionally not held during either
of the rainy seasons, nor during festivals. But as soon as
the rain dries up, and the Turas and Triple-Moon Conjunction festivals are over, I'm due back in court.

'Cicerius won't protect you forever.'

'Samilius,' I reply, with dignity, 'I don't need Cicerius
to protect me from you. As a Praetor you are about as
much use as a eunuch in a brothel, besides which you
are dumb as an Orc. Feel free to contact me any time.
Now good day.'

Kemlath meets me outside the Abode of Justice. He's
hugging his cloak round him and notices that I'm not
getting wet.

'Using one of your spells to keep dry?'

'I'm using my only spell to keep dry.'

'Your only spell? Aren't you carrying a few others to
help with your business? A couple of fighting spells and
maybe something for reading hidden documents?'

I admit that I can't really carry around more than one
or two these days. 'It's taking all my powers just to keep

dry. I don't let on how little magic I can use. How do you think my aura got on the knife?'

Kemlath isn't sure. He's well aware that Old Hasius the Brilliant is not easy to fool. 'But there are ways. I'll apply myself and see what I can come up with. Meanwhile, you'd better tell me everything. It might give me some clues as to who is attacking you.'

I'm grateful to Kemlath. We did fight together, but that was a long time ago and he doesn't owe me anything.

There are always plenty of landuses for hire in Thamlin, unlike Twelve Seas. The drivers aren't so keen to take you down there either.

'The nearest bar,' I instruct the driver. 'And then the Royal Library.'

Kemlath is surprised. 'Are you planning on some reading?'

'No, talking.'

The driver pulls up at an elegant hostelry at the edge of the sloping woodlands between the Palace grounds and Thamlin. The clientele here – senior Palace servants and officials, one or two Senators and their secretaries, even a Sorcerer or two – sit sipping wine in private alcoves. I march in, grab a waitress and instruct her to bring me their largest flagon of ale and to keep them coming till I tell her to stop.

'And food,' I add.

I used to come here to eat when I worked at the Palace. They had a good chef in those days, I hope he's still in the kitchen.

The waitress hands me a menu.

'Bring me everything. And extra bread.'

'One way of faking an aura—' begins Kemlath.

I wave him quiet. 'Too hungry. Wait.'

I down my tankard in one, start on the second and signal to the bartender to bring me another. The first courses start to arrive, bread and some fancy fish entrées. I can't scoop up enough food using the small spoon provided, so I shovel it in with my fingers and the aid of the bread.

'More beer,' I tell the waitress before she leaves. 'Quickly. And bring the next courses.'

She smiles. No doubt the staff appreciate a man with a healthy appetite. Inside the hostelry it is cool and pleasant. I haven't been this comfortable for weeks. The waitress wheels up a cart carrying six main courses and a hefty selection of side dishes. She looks at me enquiringly.

'Just leave the cart,' I tell her. 'And bring me another beer. Have you any bigger flagons?'

Kemlath looks on in some surprise as I demolish the contents of the food cart. He's sipping a glass of wine and picking at a small plate of roast fowl.

'I have to be careful with my stomach,' he says, apologetically.

That's sorcery. It can't guarantee a healthy appetite and a good digestion.

'Can I bring you anything else?' says the waitress. I tell her to bring another wagonload of main courses.

'But pile it up higher. And one of each dessert. And more bread. Did you bring me beer? Better bring another.'

I undo my belt and my sword clatters to the floor. I let it lie there and carry on eating. Some time later I'm feeling Human again.

'More beer,' I tell the waitress.

I notice the kitchen boy is peering out from the kitchen with awe on his face.

'Must be a while since they had a good eater in here,' I mutter to Kemlath, and get down to the wide range of desserts.

Later, when I'm imbibing another beer and finishing off a few scraps, the chef appears at our table.

'Thraxas!' he says, throwing his hands in the air with pleasure. 'I should have known it was you! We miss you!'

Outside the landus driver is wet as a Mermaid's blanket and looks as miserable as a Niojan whore. Landus drivers are notoriously bad-tempered.

'The Library,' I instruct.

'I've never seen such an appetite,' says Kemlath Orc Slayer admiringly, as we drive off.

'I need a lot of fuel. I've serious investigating to do. And the way I keep getting thrown in prison these days I never know when my next meal might be.'

I take a drink from the flagon of ale I brought out with me. I'll have to finish it before we enter the Royal Library. I know from experience that the curators are touchy about anyone getting too close to their books and manuscripts while carrying a flagon of ale.

'Who are you meeting?' asks Kemlath as the vast marble building comes into view.

'Makri.'

'The woman who killed the Orcs? Can she read?'

'She certainly can. And don't let her hear you doubting it. Makri's a budding intellectual and she's very touchy with men who give her a hard time about it. Apart from me, but then I taught her the skills needed to survive in the city.'

'Why do you want to see her now?'

'Because she's smart. I want to tell her what's been happening and see if she has any ideas. Also I have some good news for her.'

This is Makri's regular study time. Not surprisingly, the Library staff were taken aback when a young woman with Orc blood started to appear asking for manuscripts about philosophy and rhetoric, but as the Library extends membership to all people attending the Guild College they were obliged to let her in. Now they're used to her, the staff are pleased to see her, rather like the chef being pleased to see me: they like anyone who appreciates what they do.

I leave Kemlath in the landus after arranging to meet him in an hour at the Avenging Axe. The Royal Library is vast, with two huge wings and a massive central dome housing one of the finest collections of works in the west.

'Please leave your wet cloak in the cloakroom,' says the doorkeeper.

'Completely dry,' I say, pointing.

He looks impressed. Everything else in the city is soaking wet but I'm walking round dry and cosy. What a superb spell.

I head for the extensive philosophy section, housed in another smaller dome at the back. All around are thousands of books and manuscripts. Small busts of kings, saints and heroes are set into alcoves in the walls and the ceiling is painted with a magnificent fresco of Saint Quatinius banishing the Orcs, painted by the great Usax, the finest ever Turanian artist, who lived around a hundred years ago. That's certainly a lot of culture for one building. Makri likes it. I had never been to the place before Makri arrived in the city.

That was one reason she chose Turai. Plenty of culture. And she heard there was a lot of fighting as well. She was right on both counts, but she says she wasn't expecting us to be so degenerate. There again, she wasn't expecting to be able to earn money from her shape. She never even knew she had an impressive figure when she was a gladiator. Orcs don't find Human women attractive, so no one ever mentioned it.

I find her engrossed in some old scroll. She looks at me suspiciously.

'Have you got beer hidden somewhere?'

'Of course not.'

'You had last time. The librarian was upset.'

'Well, I haven't this time.'

'It's not very considerate, you know, Thraxas. I need to come here to study. It's been awkward for me, as you well know. The last thing I need is for you to arrive drunk and spilling beer all over the manuscripts.'

'For God's sake, Makri, I've just got out of prison. I'm on a murder charge. Will you pick some other time to lecture me about my drinking? I've got good news for you.'

A librarian in a toga strides forwards and tells me to be quiet and stop disturbing the other readers. Makri gives me a foul look then stands up and motions for me to accompany her to another small room where we can talk.

'What good news?'

'Sword of Vengeance won.'

Makri lets out a cry of pleasure and practically

dances round the table. I'm feeling smug.

'You see? Didn't I tell you I could pick winners? Easy as bribing a Senator for a man of my talents. Okay, I may have the odd bad day, but when you want some expert help with chariot racing, Thraxas is the man to come to.'

Makri tots up her winnings in her head.

'Twenty-seven gurans. And I have eighteen already – except I owe you ten – that means I now have thirty-five. Is the race meeting in Juval still on?'

'Another couple of days. If you can call in at Mox's for a form sheet I'll study it tonight.'

'The form sheet always gets wet when I walk back from Mox's,' says Makri cunningly. 'Lend me the magic dry cloak.'

I hand it over with a sigh. 'Great spell,' says Makri, wrapping it around her comfortably. 'What's happening with the murder case?'

Makri listens while I recount the latest developments. 'I still don't know anything about Lisox, that guy trying to kill Sarija. Captain Rallee says he used to work for Glixius Dragon Killer. Remember him?'

'Sure. He must be behind it all,' she says. 'He doesn't like you, and he's a Sorcerer.'

'Maybe. He's a powerful fighter, but I'm not sure his sorcery is good enough to fool Hasius the Brilliant about the murder weapon. But he could have improved. He's certainly my number one suspect.'

'Are you really in trouble?' asks Makri.

'I am. It's fairly normal for the Guards to suspect me of every crime they can't find a better suspect for, but someone is really fitting me up for this one. Even Cicerius has his doubts. If I don't crack the case soon I'm in serious trouble. I can't work out if it's all connected to the murder, or if it's more of Rittius's campaign to get me.'

Makri wonders if I have any good leads. I admit I have not. I made no progress with Carilis. I think the next step is to speak to Mursius's wife Sarija.

'I expect she'll be full of dwa again. It gets me down trying to get any sense out of dwa addicts.'

'Maybe she won't use so much dwa now she's taken responsibility for entering Mursius's chariot in the Turas Memorial.'

I'm surprised to hear Makri say this. 'How did you know about that?'

'It's all over town. The students at the college are talking about nothing else. Everyone is wondering about the race with the Elves and the Orcs. Has Sarija's chariot got any chance?'

'None at all. You weren't thinking of betting on it, were you?'

'Maybe.'

'Bet on the Elf. Unless the Orcish chariot turns out to be better than we expect. That's if the Orcish chariot runs. I haven't made any progress with the prayer mat yet. I'm hoping Cicerius can persuade some Sorcerer to find it. What are Orcs like with racing chariots, anyway? They seemed pretty handy in the war.'

'They're good,' says Makri. 'Some of them are good with horses too. I wouldn't be surprised if Rezaz the Butcher is bringing something hot to Turai.'

I notice that despite her hatred of all things Orcish even Makri is getting caught up in the excitement of the race. Before I depart I ask her if she has any suggestions for finding the prayer mat. She hasn't.

I call in on my friend Astrath Triple Moon but it's another fruitless meeting. He can't tell me anything about the bronze cup Kerk brought me.

'It's been cleaned.'

Every single thing I need to know about these days has been sorcerously tampered with. Damned Sorcerers.

I ask Astrath if he can look back in time and pick up something about the three Orcs I encountered in Ferias, but he draws a blank on that too.

'Whoever cleaned the area is too powerful for me, Thraxas,' he says, looking gloomy because he's stuck in the city in the rain along with the rest of us, and doesn't have a nice villa in Thamlin to shelter in like the other Sorcerers.

'How much would Turai's Sorcerers know about Orcs? Specifically their religion?'

'Do Orcs have a religion?' asks Astrath.

'They might have. You know, temples and bishops and things like that. And prayer mats.'

Astrath chuckles. 'I doubt it. They're too savage to spend any time praying.'

So it seems that even Sorcerers are ignorant of Orcish prayers. Someone in this city must be aware. Someone knew enough to remove the prayer mat.

Back in Twelve Seas the mood is still ugly. The Civil Guards have pacified the area, but you can feel the sullen resentment everywhere. The drinkers in the Avenging Axe mutter complaints against the King and the Consul for allowing it.

'I didn't risk my life against the Orcs just so they could run chariots at the Turas Memorial,' growls old Parax the shoemaker. His cronies nod in angry agreement.

I don't remember Parax risking his life at the time – I seem to recall he spent the war hiding in his mother's attic – but he catches the mood of the moment in the Avenging Axe. Gurd is bewildered. As a Barbarian he never had much grasp of grand strategy and stolidly subscribes to the idea of killing all Orcs on sight.

'Maybe we're just luring Rezaz here so we can ambush him,' he says hopefully.

Makri squeezes her body into her bikini but the gloom that pervades the place is bad for tips. Drinker after drinker arrives in the tavern, curses the rain, curses the Orcs and sits brooding over a flagon of ale. Even when she adopts emergency tactics of removing a couple of links from the garment, making it so small she might as well be wandering around naked, it doesn't bring much of a result.

'These copper mines might be good for the King's treasury, but it's ruining my income,' she complains, slamming a few beers down at a table full of dockers who barely glance at her before getting back to muttering to each other.

A few people ask me about my hunt for Mursius's killer. They know the Guards suspect me but, at least in the Avenging Axe, no one takes me for a murderer. I tell everybody I'm making good progress.

'Mursius knew how to treat Orcs,' says Parax. 'Fling them off the battlements, that's what you do with Orcs.'

He leaps to his feet, banging his fist on the table.

'I'd kill any man who helped an Orc!' he roars.

'We're going to be popular when news leaks out,' whispers Makri as she passes.

Kemlath arrives. His sumptuous rainbow cloak creates a minor sensation in the Avenging Axe. We don't get many high-class Sorcerers down this way. With his large frame, his jovial laugh and his collection of gold necklaces, Kemlath is hard to ignore. The jewellery alone would attract plenty of attention as no one would normally be foolish enough to walk through Twelve Seas wearing such valuable items. Kemlath is safe of course. No one is going to try and rob a Sorcerer. Not even a dwa addict would be confused enough to do that. Sorcerers Guild rules allow them to respond to personal attacks with as much force as necessary, and an angry Sorcerer might well decide it's necessary to fry you to a crisp.

He's come to get a full description of recent events and see what he can find out by sorcerous means.

'Good tavern,' he says, as I lead him upstairs. 'Can you smell burning?'

I can. There's smoke in the upstairs corridor, coming from beneath my office door. I rush in and my desk is on fire. My desk?

I run to the bucket under the sink to get water. The bucket's empty. I haven't been bringing up water for bathing these last few days. No real need, with all the rain.

'It's all right,' calls Kemlath before he utters some word of power. The fire immediately dies away. Yet again I regret not studying more when I was an Apprentice. I open the outside door and the smoke clears slowly out of my room, mingling with the steam rising from the streets outside as the sun beats down during a break in the rain.

A message is scorched on the surface in spidery, blackened letters.

Do not attempt to find the works of art, it says.

I stare at the warning. Bit of an odd message.

'It isn't easy to send a burning message like that,' muses Kemlath Orc Slayer. 'He must be a powerful Sorcerer. Or she.'

'Well, he or she is going to get a nasty shock when I catch up with them,' I growl. 'No one burns my desk and gets away with it. Do not attempt to find the works of art, indeed. I'll find them and ram them down his throat.'

Kemlath looks around, seeing if he can pick up any trace of where the attack came from. Could it be Glixius Dragon Killer? If so, he's much more skilled than he used to be. Makri said she saw him in the Royal Library last week. Perhaps he's been studying.

The smoke clears. I drink some klee and note with dissatisfaction that it's my last bottle. I now have very little money left, and every time I turn around I'm being warned, attacked, arrested and generally harassed half to death. I'm making little progress in any direction and Sarija has been sending me messages asking what I'm doing about finding Mursius's murderer. I send back a message saying I'm doing everything I can. In which case, I suppose, I'd better do something.

CHAPTER
TWELVE

Unfortunately during the week that follows I achieve very little. The rain pours down, the streets turn into rivers of mud, and I run into dead end after dead end. It's been raining for twenty-two days and I'm no nearer to finding either Mursius's killer or the Orcish prayer mat. Cicerius keeps demanding to know when I'm going to come up with something, and I'm fast running out of excuses.

I've asked representatives from every conceivable group of people in Turai what they know about Orcish religion, and the sum total is nothing at all. The Honourable Association of Merchants, the Sorcerers, the Guard, the Brotherhood, the Transport Guild, the True Church, the Goldsmiths, and plenty more besides. As far as I can see no one in Turai knows enough about Orcs to even guess they have a religion, let alone deliberately set out to steal their prayer mat. I'm starting to wonder if the whole thing is a coincidence. Maybe someone took the mat to keep their feet dry. Furthermore these questions are very bad for my reputation, with the city being so touchy about Orcs just now.

I wouldn't be floundering around in quite such a hopeless manner if Cicerius could tell me anything useful, but he can't. No one who shouldn't have been there was seen near the Prince's villa. And when Old Hasius the Brilliant gets round to checking the scene, he can't find anything.

'How is it that Sorcerers can never find anything?' I complain loudly to Makri. 'The damned city is top heavy with Sorcerers yet every time there's a crime and I could use a little help there's nothing they can do. Either the moons are in the wrong conjunction or the whole area's been mysteriously cleaned up. What's the point of having so many Sorcerers if all they can do is make up horoscopes for handmaidens? It's not like that when I get accused of something, of course. No chance. Then it's, "We found Thraxas's aura on the knife so let's throw him in the slammer." I tell you, Makri, they're useless. Damned Sorcerers. I hate them.'

'What about Kemlath?'

I admit I don't hate Kemlath. At least he's trying to be helpful. He keeps hanging round anyway, though I think there might be more to it than helping me.

'I think he's taken a shine to Sarija,' I say.

'Sarija? Wouldn't he regard her as beneath him? And kindly don't turn that into one of your crude jokes.'

'Who knows? Sorcerers aren't quite as hidebound about that sort of thing as other aristocrats. And Kemlath comes from the far west originally, same as Astrath. He's certainly been spending a lot of time with her. Says he's helping her to kick dwa.'

Makri agrees that this does seem to be working. 'But that might be because you got her addicted to beer instead.'

'Well it's far healthier. Build her up. She'll need her

energy if she's still planning to enter Storm the Citadel in the Turas Memorial.'

I stare glumly out of the window. Magic dry cloak or not, I can hardly bear going out in the rain again. Yesterday the aqueduct that runs down to Twelve Seas collapsed with the weight of water. Workers sent by the local branch of the Revered Federation of Guilds are now struggling to repair it. The guilds are blaming Prefect Drinius for the lack of maintenance. The Prefect is accusing the guilds of inflating their workmen's fees. Strikes and litigation are threatened on all sides. It's standard Hot Rainy Season stuff, and adds to the general gloom.

Kerk's seller of stolen goods claims to know nothing of the bronze cup. He has no more of the works of art and won't even admit that the cup came from his shop. His business is under the protection of the Brotherhood so there's little I can do to threaten him. I ask Kerk to notify me if anything else comes on to the market.

Neither Astrath or Kemlath could learn anything from the cup, and I'm no further on with the murder of Mursius. Even though Sarija is my client I haven't neglected to have her checked out, or Carilis. Nothing useful turns up. Close questioning of servants, relatives, local shopkeepers and various others fails to reveal if Carilis was having an affair with Senator Mursius. Some think she might have been. Others don't. No one knows for sure. And even if she was, so what? There's nothing particularly unusual in a Senator having an affair with another woman. If that woman is young, attractive and engaged in looking after the dwa-ridden shell of Mursius's wife, it seems quite probable, but no reason for a man to get murdered. Even if his wife Sarija was the jealous type, I doubt she could have stayed on her feet long enough to do it.

Carilis has gone to ground and refuses to speak to me. She won't tell me how she knew where the goods were. I think she's scared.

I've no idea why Mursius was in the warehouse in the first place. No one reports any strange behaviour on his part and his personal attendant claims not to know what he did that day.

'The Senator gave me the day off,' he tells me. Very convenient for him, if not for me.

Guardsman Jevox tells me that the Civil Guard still thinks I'm the culprit. Even so, it's carrying on with its investigations under pressure from Rittius and Samilius, trying to dig up more evidence to nail me. They haven't turned up anything new. This gives *The Renowned Chronicle* something to whine about, though it spends most of its time complaining about the imminent arrival of the Orcish chariot. The city is still simmering. The True Church is particularly upset and its Pontifexes thunder against the notion from their pulpits. Even Archbishop Xerius, a strong supporter of the King, lets it be known in private that he's not happy.

I do turn up one interesting fact. Drasius the banker wasn't the only one to hear the rumour about the Society of Friends planning a major betting coup on the Turas Memorial. The story has certainly passed around town among the betting fraternity. This doesn't prove anything – such rumours are common enough among Turai's perpetually paranoid gamblers – but it's interesting if only because Glixius Dragon Killer is a known associate of the Society. A man of his sorcerous power might be expected to be in on the plot. I've received two more sorcerous warnings, presumably from Glixius, so I'm interested in anything he does right now.

I wonder about the Turas Memorial. Even though Senator Mursius knew the Elves were entering, he advised me to back Storm the Citadel with everything I had. Why was he so confident? Could he possibly have been involved in the plot somehow? Might the Society of Friends have been planning to help Storm the Citadel win? I doubt it but I can't absolutely dismiss it. Nor can I dismiss the other possibility, that Mursius just stumbled into the picture somehow and was murdered by the Society to keep him quiet. Nothing really points that way, however.

I sit downstairs with a flagon of ale in front of me.

Makri brings me another as she finishes her shift. She notices that my face fails to light up as the beer arrives.

'No progress?'

'Nothing.'

'Can I borrow the magic dry cloak for College tonight?'

'Okay.'

'Really?'

'I've no use for it. I've investigated everything and found nothing. I'm just going to sit here drinking till Praetor Samilius comes and arrests me for the murder.'

'When will that be?'

'Probably right before Glixius kills me with a spell.'

'Come on, Thraxas,' says Makri. 'There's no point sitting round being as miserable as a Niojan whore about everything.'

'Fine,' I say. 'You have cheered me immensely. I am now as happy as a drunken mercenary.'

'Don't get angry with me,' says Makri.

Makri is easily annoyed these days. The constant downpour, the strain of her studies and the amount of shifts she has to work are getting to her. And she still hasn't collected the sixty gurans she promised Minarixa. The race meeting in Juval ended without us finding another chariot worth backing. Makri asked Gurd for a loan, but Gurd's trade has been poor and he's also had the expense of fixing the roof, which sprang several leaks in one of last week's storms. So he claims, anyway, though I suspect that Gurd may just be unwilling to lend out any money for the purposes of helping the Association of Gentlewomen. In the northern Barbarian lands where Gurd comes from, women have a lower social status than horses, and he finds it difficult to adapt to our more civilised ways.

Makri's only hope of raising the sixty in time is at another race meet even further south in Simnia. She's frustrated with the delay. In truth sixty gurans isn't going to get the Association of Gentlewomen very far. They've run into problems with their attempt to have themselves recognised by the Revered Federation Council. They need money to pay a bribe to the Praetor in charge of Guild Affairs and they need it quickly else the whole process will be delayed for a year. The local group has been going round Twelve Seas with collection boxes and getting precious little reward for their troubles. Maybe the rich women up in Thamlin are doing better. Lisutaris, Mistress of the Sky, is a member, I believe. She's a very powerful Sorcerer.

'Get Lisutaris to magic you some money,' I suggest to Makri.

'Could she do that?' asks Makri, eagerly.

'Of course not,' I reply, having a good laugh at Makri's naïveté.

Makri storms off annoyed. I never like to let a day pass without upsetting someone, as my ex-wife used to say. I gather up another beer and slump back in my chair.

Parax the shoemaker stumbles through the door.

'Goddamn it, I'm wet,' he says. 'It's the Orcs.'

Parax is a fool. It's day twenty-two of the Hot Rainy Season. He knows as well as everyone else that there's another eight days to go, Orcs or no Orcs. Gurd points this out to him.

'Well, it's heavier than usual,' counters Parax, continuing to insist that we're cursed. I wonder what he'd say if he knew that Rezaz the Butcher was here already.

I study the form for the chariots in the upcoming meeting in Simnia. Far south of Turai, it's hot there. Too hot, really, but at least they don't have a Hot Rainy Season. I wish I was there just now, far away from this damp, stinking, corrupt and crime-ridden city.

I turn the sheet of paper listing the chariots over to study the other side. Except on the other side there don't seem to be any chariots. Just a message printed in red ink: *Take care, Thraxas, you have little time left*.

I slam it down in a fury. This has gone too far. Now I can't even read the racing form without a sorcerous warning appearing and messing it up.

Kemlath Orc Slayer arrives later in the day and I show him the message.

'Can't you pick up anything from it?'

So far Kemlath has been unable to say for sure where any of the sorcerous warnings have come from. He stares hard at the document for a long time.

'I think he's getting careless,' says Kemlath, eventually. 'I wouldn't stake my reputation on it in a court of law, but I think this message has faint traces of Glixius Dragon Killer on it.'

I pound the table. 'So! It is Glixius! He's trying to scare me off the investigation.'

Kemlath, as ever, is wearing plenty of jewellery: gold chains, silver bracelets, and a distinctive antique ring on his finger with a fabulous blue stone in it. He buys me a beer and asks how the case is going. I tell him I've made little progress.

'I can't seem to get a handle on it somehow. But I'm still hopeful more of Mursius's art will turn up. If the cup did, there's no reason why a few more pieces shouldn't find their way on to the market. Once they do, it might give me an opening.'

'Do you think the same person that stole the works of art murdered Mursius?'

'Probably. Either that or they know who did.'

'You think it's Glixius?'

I nod. 'He's never been convicted of anything. Thinks he's safe with his sorcery and his aristocratic connections. Well, he's wrong. If he killed Mursius, I'm going to nail him.'

'You were always a dogged soldier,' says Kemlath, which I take as a compliment, along with another beer.

Three days later, I'm beginning to wonder if Parax might have been right about us being cursed. The rain is heavier than anyone can ever remember. Usually there are periods where it stops, the sun shines and the city gets a chance to breath. This year the downpour is relentless. Life in Twelve Seas becomes unbearable. Quintessence Street is a sea of mud and some of the small streets running off it are completely impassable. A few cheap tenements have crumbled to the ground, their foundations undermined. Everywhere you look someone is desperately trying to shore up a building, repair a roof or bail themselves out of trouble. Trade in the city slows to a crawl and the anger about the Orcs lies over Turai in a simmering cloud.

All the while the heat produces thunderstorms so terrifying that our more nervous citizens start looking up old prophesies, wondering if the end of the world might be nigh. Makri shakes her sword angrily at the sky while practising her fighting skills in the back yard in defiance of the elements.

I receive another warning. This time it's magically etched into my own flagon, which I take as a very personal attack. I'm late with the rent but for once Gurd understands that there's nothing much I can do about it. I'm not the only one finding it hard to earn a living these days. Street vendors, messengers, whores, wagon drivers – all give up the struggle with the elements and huddle indoors, waiting for it to pass.

'I've tramped over half this city looking for that damned prayer mat,' I tell Makri. 'It's one of the most frustrating cases I've ever come across.'

'What about Mursius's murder?'

'That's one of the most frustrating cases I've ever come across as well. Do you know—'

'Yes, fine,' interrupts Makri. 'So, who are we betting on in the first race at Simnia?'

'Thank you for your support. Okay, the first race in Simnia. I reckon the second favourite in the first race is a reasonable bet.'

'Only a reasonable bet? I'm running out of excuses for Minarixa. Everyone was looking at me at last night's meeting. Do you think they know I gambled the money away?'

'I doubt it. Who would suspect you, an escaped slave gladiator with Orcish blood in her veins, of acting with anything except impeccable honesty?'

We leave for Mox's.

'You might lend me the magic dry cloak.'

'No. It's mine. Who is it has to say a spell over it every day?'

I have my own reasons for needing a win at the races. I'm running severely short of money and soon won't have enough for my daily supply of beer.

'I can't function without beer.'

'Aren't you the person who always ridicules these dwa addicts for wasting their lives on a stupid drug?'

'That's not the same thing at all,' I inform my smart young companion. 'Beer is a normal healthy part of any man's diet, particularly a vigorous man like myself. It's part of our culture and heritage. Dwa is for degenerates. Let's go.'

We walk out into the swamp that used to be Quintessence Street. A gale is blowing the storm in from the sea. The rain lashes into my face and the lightning splits the sky above. I grit my teeth and struggle on. Mox's is close to the harbour, right next to Prisox's pawn shop, another establishment with which I am very familiar. Despite the adverse weather, it will be business as usual there. Prisox always has a healthy supply of sad customers trying to raise a little cash for life's necessities.

Makri, after her initial inclination to splash out on wild bets on chariots with long odds, has settled into a careful strategy and is content to go along with my suggestion of a modest gamble on Bear Baiter. She bets fifteen of her thirty-five gurans. As Bear Baiter is quoted at evens, she stands to win fifteen gurans, which will bring her close to her target. I bet a similar amount.

As we leave we run into a throng of people. The crowd seems quite cheerful, or as cheerful as it's possible to be when lightning is searing the rooftops and wind and rain are pinning you to the walls.

'What's happening?' I yell to the nearest passer-by.

'Elves are coming in,' he roars back, above the din.

Of course. The Elvish chariot is due to land at the docks today. Everyone is heading for the harbour. I can't miss this. Like any true gambler I want to see the Elvish chariot and horses in order to form some opinions of their chances in the race. And it's not just gambling that brings people here. Everyone likes Elves and Lord Lisith-ar-Moh is still a hero in Turai.

At the harbour crowds of people are straining their eyes for the first sight of the Elvish ship, and a podium has been set up for welcoming speeches. No one seems worried that the Elves might not arrive on schedule. They're renowned for their sailing skills, and have probably used sorcery to calm the waters on the way. Sure enough, a cry goes up that there's a sail on the horizon. A pleasant ripple of anticipation runs through the crowd. Everyone forgets their rain-soaked misery as the green sails gradually grow in size as the Elvish ship approaches the harbour.

Cheers go up as the Elves take down the sails and manoeuvre into the harbour. A bigger cheer goes up when Lord Lisith-ar-Moh himself is spotted on deck. He has a silver band around his brow, and his green cloak flaps in the wind. Around him are various attendants, all tall and fair. As the ship draws into the pier Elvish sailors wave to the crowd.

Elves are always tall, fair and golden-eyed. They generally wear green. Their ears are slightly pointed at the top. It's never difficult to recognise an Elf. It cheers me to see them. It cheers me further to think that if the Orcish chariot is given any chance by the bookmakers, the odds on the Elves might just stretch out far enough to be worth a bet.

Consul Kalius, Turai's most important official, is here to welcome the Elves on behalf of the King. He's standing on a podium with an attendant holding an umbrella over his head but with the storm still raging he cuts his speech short, simply welcoming the Elves to the city, thanking them for their help in the past, wishing them good luck in the race, then departing with Lord Lisith in a convoy of official carriages. The crowd applaud, and crane their necks to see the chariot being unloaded. The horses snort apprehensively as they are lowered in harnesses from the ship to the pier, but their Elvish grooms call to them, calming them down, before leading them off to the shelter of a nearby warehouse. I note with interest that this is the same warehouse in which Senator Mursius was murdered.

Do the Elves who have just arrived know they're going to be up against an Orc? I wonder. I follow as young Elves wheel their chariot into the warehouse. They're lithe and strong and show no ill effects from their long voyage through rough seas from the Southern Islands to Turai.

Makri has remained silent throughout all this activity. When it comes to Elves she has mixed emotions. She's always attracted to Elves, partly because she is quarter Elf herself and partly because she thinks that the men in Turai are such scum. On the other hand, Elves annoy the hell out of her because they always react badly to her quarter-Orc blood.

The chariot is loaded safely into the warehouse. I'm right up at the doors, peering in past the attendants. I slip past an Elf distracted by the sight of Makri and poke my head in the door. I can't believe it's a coincidence that the Elf chariot is being stored in the same place that Mursius was murdered.

Civil Guards are in attendance to keep order and to prevent anyone from touching the chariot. One of them spots me, and calls to me to get out.

'What do you think you're doing?'

'Nothing,' I grunt, though this is not quite true. In reality I'm staring at the wall of the warehouse where I've just noticed, scratched in tiny letters close to the floor, a pair of clasped hands, very crudely drawn. Just a piece of graffiti, a common enough sight in the city.

But not that particular sign, I muse, as the Guards eject me and the rest of the overly curious crowd. Two clasped hands is the sign of the Society of Friends, who don't hang around in Twelve Seas, which is controlled by the Brotherhood, their deadly enemies. Any known Society man wandering around in Twelve Seas would soon end up dead. But who else other than a Society of Friends man would make such a mark? With the Brotherhood being so powerful in the south of the city, it's not the sort of thing that even a bored youth would do. Scrawling Society of Friends graffiti is liable to earn you a good beating, or worse.

Outside Makri is talking to a young Elf in Elvish. The heavy rain has flattened her hair so her pointed ears show through. The Elf looks intrigued but troubled. Soon an Elf commander calls to him and he hurries away.

I tell Makri about the Society of Friends graffiti. Has the Society been in the warehouse in which Mursius was murdered? The same place in which the Elvish horses and chariot are now being stored prior to removal to the stables at the Stadium?

'Are you coming home, or do you want to hang around waiting for more Elves to appear?'

'Stupid Elves,' says Makri, walking rapidly away. The crowd make optimistic noises about the Orc curse being lifted now that Lord Lisith has arrived. I catch up with Makri. She's in a bad mood after meeting the Elves. Poor Makri. They're never going to welcome her like a long-lost sister.

At the end of Quintessence Street I sense magic close by and spin around in case I'm under attack. Right behind me a tall man in a grey cloak is approaching through the rain. His face looks down towards the ground but I recognise him anyway. It's Glixius Dragon Killer. I grab him as he passes, which is rash, given Glixius's power, but I'm still annoyed at the damage to my own personal tankard. He looks up in surprise.

'Leave your rainbow cloak at home, did you?'

'Thraxas! How dare you lay a hand on me. Do you wish to be blasted into the next world?'

'How dare you send me sorcerous warnings!' I counter. 'That tankard was very dear to me. And I don't appreciate you writing all over my racing form either.'

'Have you gone insane?' roars the Sorcerer. 'I have no time for your petty stupidities. Be gone!'

He raises his arm to cast some spell at me. I brace myself, hoping that my spell protection charm is in good working order. I don't get to find out because before Glixius can utter a word Makri slugs him on the back of his head with the pommel of her sword. He slumps unconscious to the ground.

'Nice work, Makri.'

'I needed that,' she says, and looks a little more cheerful. We leave Glixius lying in the mud.

'That'll teach him to meddle with me.'

At the Avenging Axe four Civil Guards and a Praetor's assistant are waiting for me. The official hands me a paper and informs me I'm due in court the day after the Triple-Moon Conjunction festival ends.

'Care to buy me a beer to celebrate?' I ask the Praetor's assistant.

He doesn't care. They depart.

'Have they charged you with the murder?' enquires Makri.

'Not exactly. Cicerius managed to have that delayed. I have to go before the examining magistrate, who looks at the evidence.'

'What happens then?'

'Then he charges me with murder.'

Later in the day I receive the news that Bear Baiter romped home a clear winner, which gives me enough money for a few beers and Makri another fifteen gurans to add to her total. She now has fifty and needs only ten more.

'Stop sitting around drinking beer,' says Makri, interrupting my late-night relaxation. 'Start studying the form sheet.'

I sigh. Life was easier when Makri disapproved of gambling. Cicerius's Aedile, or Assistant, arrives on horseback looking for news. The Deputy Consul is extremely agitated at my lack of progress in locating the prayer mat. Lord Rezaz Caseg is increasingly unhappy at his charioteer's loss and may quit the city any day. I tell the Aedile I'm doing everything I can. I have a beer in one hand and the racing sheet in the other which might give him the wrong impression. He doesn't look too impressed when he rides away.

CHAPTER
THIRTEEN

I make no progress in the next few days. I'm sitting gloomily at my desk, beer in hand, when I hear voices in the corridor outside. Makri's voice and another one, softer. I creep over and place my ear to the door. The other voice belongs to Hanama. Another social call from the Assassin?

'I won fifteen gurans on Bear Baiter,' Makri is telling her. 'Evens favourite at Simnia. He won by three lengths after a slow start. But Bear Baiter always starts slowly. I wasn't worried.'

'I didn't know you were so informed about betting,' says Hanama, sounding impressed.

'I picked it up here and there,' replies Makri. 'If you come to the Turas Memorial I'll show you how it's done.'

I wrench open the door. 'Will you stop discussing gambling with Assassins outside my room? I'm trying to work in here.'

'So, what's eating you?' asks Makri.

'Her,' I retort, indicating Hanama. 'You might be buddies, but she still gives me the creeps. Since when have Assassins placed bets? Shouldn't you be out murdering people?'

Hanama eyes me calmly and retreats down the corridor without comment, followed by Makri. Damned

Assassins. How come she's so friendly with Makri recently?

'And it was me that picked Bear Baiter,' I yell after them.

I get out the magic dry cloak. It's time to visit the Brotherhood. They are very powerful in Turai. They started off as a bunch of small-time crooks operating round the harbour about two hundred years ago. Now they're one of the most powerful groups in the whole city-state. Since dwa started flooding into the city, bringing with it vast profits and a whole new class of people dependent on crime, their influence has grown alarmingly. They're behind most criminal activity in the south of the city, but they also have their fingers in various legitimate businesses. Many of our banking houses, for instance, are now suspected of using dwa money to fund their enterprises, and when a Senator makes a speech in favour of some particular venture you can never be sure if he isn't being heavily influenced by the vast wealth and influence of the Brotherhood.

While I am too small-time to really irritate the Brotherhood, I couldn't claim that they like me. Casax, their boss in Twelve Seas, was particularly displeased with me when I prevented him from making off with the King's gold which had originally been stolen by Galwinius, our ex-Prefect. He warned me then to stay well out of his way. So some might say it is unwise of me to walk into the Mermaid, Twelve Seas' most dangerous tavern and local Brotherhood headquarters, and demand to see him.

Several thugs confer with each other then send a message upstairs. Karlox, a huge bruiser whom I have had several run-ins with in the past, appears at the top and motions me up. He shows me into the large room at the back, where Casax is sitting at a table. I greet him politely and take a seat without waiting to be asked.

He stares at me silently for a few minutes. The table is huge, beautifully carved. On the walls around us are valuable tapestries showing scenes from Turai's legendary past. Casax is not especially ostentatious as gang chiefs go but he needs to remind visitors of his power.

'Didn't I tell you to stay well out of my way, Investigator?' he says eventually.

'Probably,' I reply. 'But most people say that to me, one time or another.'

'So what do you want?'

'A chat about the Society of Friends.'

This gets his attention. The Society operate way out of my territory. I have no contacts there and no real means of gaining information about them, so I'm hoping that I might learn something from the Brotherhood. Even though they don't like me, they like the Society a lot less.

'Well?' says Casax.

I can feel Karlox's eyes boring into the back of my neck. Last time we met I was on a horse and I rode him down. He'd like to repay the compliment.

'I think they've been working down at the docks. I wondered if you might know anything about it.'

'Since when have the Brotherhood discussed their affairs with cheap Investigators?'

'I'm not asking you to discuss your affairs. I'm talking about the Society of Friends. I take it you don't know anything about the warehouse where Mursius was killed?'

I tell him about my suspicions that the Society have been at work in the warehouse. Casax asks if I have any evidence apart from the graffiti.

'No. But it all fits, more or less. You've heard the rumours that the Society are planning some sort of betting coup. Senator Mursius was entering his chariot in the Turas Memorial. His stolen artworks ended up at that warehouse. And then he ended up there too, dead. And now it turns out to be the same warehouse where the Elvish chariot is stored in when it's brought off the ship. I don't know what that all means, but it seems like too much of a coincidence to me.'

Casax ponders my words. Like all Brotherhood chiefs he's capable of brutality, but he's not dumb. If the Society has been operating secretly in his territory he wants to know all about it.

'So, what do you want from me, Investigator?'

'Information. In exchange for what I've told you. Anything you know or find out about the warehouse. And I'll tell you anything else I learn about the Society working in Twelve Seas.'

Casax remains silent for a time. The only sound is the rain beating down outside. Finally he nods. 'Okay.' He looks at me intently. 'I hear you've not been doing too well at the races.'

Casax wants me to be impressed that he knows my business. I shrug, and don't look impressed.

'You're not going to be a popular man in this city,' he continues. 'No one's going to like the man who's looking after the Orcs.'

This is a blow. I curse silently. I suppose it was bound to leak out eventually. I can't entirely hide my discomfiture.

Casax smiles; at least, the tiny twitching of his lips is probably meant to be a smile. Karlox shows me out.

'I'll kill you one day, fat man,' he says as a parting shot.

I don't bother replying. I receive too many death threats to be always coming up with smart answers.

The rain is heavier than ever. It's almost the end of the Hot Rainy Season. The water in Quintessence Street is deep enough to drown dogs and small children. There are far too many dogs and small children around here anyway. It takes me a long time to walk back to the Avenging Axe. Sweat pours down inside my cloak. The Hot Rainy Season. I hate it. I thank God that this is the last day. Tomorrow, according to Turai's regular calendar, the rain will dry up and we'll have a month or so of pleasant autumn weather before winter arrives.

The prospect of the rain ending has restored some cheer to the inhabitants of Turai, but it's overshadowed by the knowledge that this is also the day that the Orcish chariot is due to arrive. As the land route from the east is impassable at this time of year they'll be coming by sea like the Elves, though without the welcoming reception party. Twelve Seas is crawling with Civil Guards, posted to keep order. Even though this is the King's idea he's not going to risk lowering himself in public opinion by officially greeting the Orcs, and even Consul Kalius seems to be distancing himself. The only officials there to greet them will be Cicerius and Melus the Fair, Stadium Sorcerer.

I practically bump into Captain Rallee at the foot of my stairs. 'Don't expect the Guards to protect you over this one,' he says.

'I take it you've heard the news.'

'I have. Never thought I'd see the day when you'd be guarding Orcs, Thraxas.'

'Me neither.'

'Why are you doing it?'

I explain to the Captain upstairs in my office. He understands how I've been forced into it, but he doesn't think that your average Turanian will have much sympathy. 'The way the scandal sheets will report it you'll have volunteered for the job.'

The Captain crosses over to the window and stares out at the rain. 'Last day, thank God,' he mutters. I ask him if he'll be putting in an appearance at the Avenging Axe tonight. There's always a prolonged celebration on the night of the last day of the Hot Rainy Season and the Captain's not averse to a spot of celebrating himself. He shakes his head.

'I'm on duty. They've cancelled all leave. The city's restless. The rain's been keeping the lid on, but no one's happy about the Orcs coming. I don't like the way things are shaping up, Thraxas. Too many strange things are happening. You know it's rumoured the Society of Friends are planning some sort of betting coup?'

'Yeah, I heard.'

'You know I even heard a whisper that the Assassins are placing bets? It's like some sort of fever's gripped the city since it was learned the Elves and the Orcs are coming.'

The Captain tosses down the rest of his klee, fastens his cloak and departs abruptly. Melus the Fair is going to have to be in good form to keep things legal. Talking of Melus the Fair, she's due back in town today. She's been away out west on a goodwill mission to study sorcery in Samsarina. She's due to welcome the Orcish chariot into town.

There's a knock at the door. I answer it with a sword in my hand, ready for anything. It turns out to be a bedraggled messenger who hands over a scroll then departs. I unroll it and read it:

Found more artwork, it says. Kerk's signature is at the bottom. Good. At last something is going well.

Makri arrives. 'Are we going to Mox's?'

'Sure you don't want to go with your Assassin friend?' I say.

Makri doesn't rise to the bait. We sneak down Quintessence Street, which isn't too difficult as the torrential downpour cuts visibility almost to zero. We're sneaking because Minarixa the baker is annoyed at Makri for failing to come up with the sixty gurans as promised.

'I've really offended the Association of Gentlewomen. It's hell. Last night Chulani the carpet-weaver said very pointedly that she was surprised to hear that certain members had been gambling with the Association's money and was Minarixa planning to do anything about running these members out of Turai.'

'She might not have been referring to you,' I point out. 'Half the city is gripped by gambling fever just now. You're probably not the only member of the A.G. who's diverted funds to the bookies.'

'I'm sure someone's been spreading rumours.'

'Well don't look at me. The only contact I have with the Association of Gentlewomen is my daily order for two large meat pies and three loaves of bread at Minarixa's bakery. Face it, Makri, you haven't been that discreet. Anyone could have seen you hanging round Honest Mox's.'

Makri screws up her face in near anguish. 'How did I ever get into this?' she demands, staring accusingly at me.

We're on our way to place a bet before joining in the welcoming committee for the Orcish chariot. Makri's fifty gurans have shrunk to thirty, the result of a very poor performance by the favourite in the last race in Simnia. Makri spent most of the evening cursing all horses, chariots and race meetings and demanded to know if the Sorcerer at Simnia is honest.

'If I find he's been taking bribes I'll ride down to Simnia myself and gut him like a pig,' she raged. More or less standard behaviour for any gambler in Turai. It gets into the blood somehow. The streets are thick with Civil Guards and the Palace has sent down wagonloads of troops to back them up in case serious trouble erupts.

I sense a certain coldness in the air as Makri and I enter Mox's. News of my cursed mission must be spreading.

'Just can't keep away from Orcs,' whispers someone.

'He's brought one with him,' whispers someone else.

Makri's eyes widen and her hand flashes to her sword as she prepares to wreak mayhem for being called an Orc, but she remembers what she's doing here and checks herself. She needs to win another thirty gurans urgently and she's not going to be able to do that if she destroys Mox's shop and everyone in it. She's tense enough already at the bet she's putting on. Victory or Death is even money but is only joint favourite and I'm not at all certain about its chances. Makri, however, has no choice. She's run out of time and must now place her whole remaining thirty gurans on the chariot and hope it comes in a winner.

'Shame you haven't found the prayer mat, Thraxas. I'd have given it a try.'

We wait at the queue. The man in front of me, a large, ugly individual I've never seen before, suddenly turns to me and snarls 'Orc lover' right in my face.

Like Makri, I hold myself back. I don't want to get into a fight, not before I've placed a bet.

'Merely helping the King out,' I answer pleasantly. It doesn't placate him. I draw myself up and try to look like a Sorcerer who might just blast everyone to hell if they're not careful. This sometimes works, as most people in Twelve Seas don't realise how insignificant my powers really are. Many hostile eyes follow me as I advance up the queue. At the counter Mox is sullen. Despite the fact that I've been one of his finest customers for years he refuses to greet me, and takes my bet in silence.

Outside the shop I hurry away, with Makri at my heels.

'This is bad. Damn that Cicerius.'

Makri is bristling about her treatment. She says that if her chariot doesn't win she's going to go back and kill everyone in Mox's for daring to call her an Orc.

'What if it wins?'

'I'll let some of them live.'

I figure I might as well take a look at the Orcish chariot that's causing me so much grief. The rain beats down and another storm rolls in off the sea. By the time we reach the harbour the sky is black and the crowd is wailing that we're cursed.

'God will destroy us for welcoming them into the city,' yells a young Pontifex, who urges the crowd to repent while they still have the chance.

Visibility is so poor that the Orcish ship is not seen until its monstrous black sails suddenly loom out of the darkness right at the mouth of the harbour. The mob yells in fury and the Civil Guards and soldiers struggle to keep order. Thunder roars in one long continuous explosion and the rain batters down like hailstones from hell. As the ship draws slowly alongside the pier Lord Rezaz Caseg and his attendants suddenly appear to welcome their fellow Orcs. His black cloak billows in the wind. His features are hidden by a black and gold helmet. The crowd explode with rage and the soldiers beat them back with staffs.

Suddenly, at the podium set up for the welcoming committee, green and blue shafts of light cut through the air. The shafts grow in intensity before bursting into star shapes which float over the heads of the crowd. They hang in the rain-darkened atmosphere before changing again into huge yellow flowers which slowly drift off towards the clouds. The crowd stop rioting, their attention drawn by the fine pyrotechnic display.

Melus the Fair steps forward on to the podium, her staff in her hand. I have my own illuminated staff with me, hanging from my belt. It's pretty feeble compared with Melus's. The crowd applaud. Melus the Fair is a popular favourite. As she raises her hands, the crowd becomes almost peaceful and the Orcs begin to disembark without trouble.

'Nice trick, ' I mutter to Makri. 'Lets hope she's in as good form at the Turas Memorial.'

We all watch as Lord Rezaz removes his helmet and marches forward, flanked by eight warrior Orcs, to meet Melus. Cicerius has now appeared at her side and he holds his hand up, palm outwards, in formal greeting. I notice that Melus has put a magic dry spell on her cloak, which is the smart thing to do, but poor old Cicerius is getting very wet indeed. His toga clings to his bony frame.

The crowd watch, partly in anger and partly in fascination. Many of our younger citizens have never even seen an Orc before. The Orc Lord marches with more dignity than I would have credited, and greets his compatriots and Melus. Speeches are extremely brief. Everyone knows this is not an occasion to spend too much time over.

Lord Rezaz mutters an order that is transmitted from his attendants to the crew of the ship. A huge covered crate is lowered from the ship to the pier. The Orc chariot. Attendants are strapping the Orc steeds into the harnesses they use at the docks for unloading livestock.

To the disappointment of the crowd, the chariot is drawn into the warehouse without being uncovered. Now that the Orcs are here, and trouble has been kept at bay, not a few of the onlookers are keen for a sight of the chariot, if only to help them judge which way to bet. The horses look impressive enough – large and jet black, with fiery eyes and long manes, groomed to perfection.

'They're here,' says a voice in my ear.

It's Kemlath. This must be very strange for him. One of Turai's most notable killers of Orcs, and he's forced to watch them arriving in the city as guests of the King.

Melus, Cicerius and the Orcs quickly depart in a string of carriages. The soldiers advance to clear away the crowds. We make our way back to the Avenging Axe via Honest Mox's.

As soon as I step inside I know we've lost our bets. I can always tell. I glance at the board on which Mox has just chalked up the result, fresh up from the Sorcerer in Simnia. Victory or Death lost by a short head.

Makri's head droops. We make to leave.

'Been seeing your Orcish friends up at the harbour?' sneers a large docker with arms like tree trunks and fists to match. Makri spins on her heel so fast it's hard to catch exactly what she does but at the end of it her elbow is sunk about eight inches into the docker's stomach. His mouth opens. No sound comes out and he collapses to the floor. Makri walks out slowly and with dignity. I hurry after her. Kemlath is impressed.

'Fine technique,' he says, but Makri is in too bad a mood to acknowledge the compliment. Instead she curses the rain.

'It'll be sunny tomorrow,' I say.

'But I still won't have any money,' says Makri. 'I can't believe I went through all that and I'm back where I started. These chariot races are fixed.'

A woman with a basket appears through the gloom and Makri hurls herself down an alleyway out of sight.

'Member of the A.G.?' I enquire, after she's gone.

'Coxi the fishwife. Very militant.'

We make our way home through the impossible mud. I offer Makri my magic dry cloak but she says she's so wet already it doesn't matter.

CHAPTER
FOURTEEN

Two messages are waiting for me at the Avenging Axe. One of them, etched in magical letters of fire on my front door, says: *Beware, your death approaches*. Now I'll have to get the door repainted. At least the rain put the fire out.

The other one is from Cicerius. In it he informs me that Lord Rezaz is again threatening to leave the city if he doesn't get his charioteer's prayer mat back quickly. Now his chariot is here he wants to practise.

I curse. This is the last night of the Hot Rainy Season. Everyone celebrates. Can't they leave a man in peace for one day? How am I meant to find their damned prayer mat? If it's so important to these Orcs, why did they lose it in the first place? Cicerius tells me that it'll be another couple of weeks until the moons are in the correct alignment for Old Hasius to check back in time. That's no use to anyone.

I'm uptown, wondering what to do next. I have a couple of beers in a small tavern frequented by the young apprentices from the local silversmith. Inspiration fails to strike. I decide to visit Makri in the Library. Maybe she'll have some good ideas. I find her sitting with a bundle of old scrolls, but she is too disconsolate about losing her money to have any good ideas.

'Last day of the rain. Major celebration tonight.'

'I don't feel like celebrating,' replies Makri.

'Neither do I.'

A bearded scholar at the next table looks at us point-edly and we lower our voices. I glance at the scroll in front of Makri. It's entitled *Comparative Religion* and is some deathly dull treatise on the subtle differences between religious practices in Turai and its neighbours. We pray three times a day in Turai. In Nioj it's six. In Mattesh it's four. Fascinating stuff.

A germ of an idea appears. I lean forward to whisper to Makri. 'Would this library have anything about Orc religion?'

Makri doesn't know. 'If anything has ever been written about it, it'll be here. Why?'

'Sudden Investigator's intuition,' I tell her.

There's a very large and comprehensive catalogue, which Makri, with her superior knowledge, starts check-ing. After a fair amount of shuttling back and forth between various volumes, she finally locates a relevant entry.

'There is a scroll about Orcish religion. Just one. Written in the last century by some scholar I've never heard of.'

Makri leads me to the centre of the library where the librarians sit behind a large counter decorated with paintings of the saints, most of whom seem to be reading manuscripts. She approaches a young man and asks him for the scroll. He blushes, then goes off to find it.

'He has a crush on me,' whispers Makri.

He's gone a long time. When he finally returns he's carrying a small scroll, the entire sum of knowledge in

Turai about Orcish religion. I take it to a table and start to unroll it. The scroll is dusty with age, but I notice that some of the dust has recently been shifted.

'Here. Chapter Three. Prayer mats.'

It's a very full description of the role of prayer mats in the Orcish Lands. I read it through.

'The importance extends to the class of charioteers who will not ride their chariot unless standing firmly on their mat. Failure to do so would mean they risked being sent to the place of damnation should they die in an accident whilst riding. Well, how about that?'

I ask Makri to enquire of the young librarian if anyone has borrowed this scroll recently. I see him blushing, and then sorting through some records. Makri comes back to the table.

'Pontifex Derlex,' she says. 'He borrowed it last week. As far as the librarian can tell, he's the first person to look at it in fifty years.'

I rise to my feet. 'A sudden breakthrough.'

'Looks like it,' agrees Makri. 'What made you think of it?'

'Intuition. Some days it's sharp as an Elf's ear. Let's go.'

Makri leaves the library with me. She can't concentrate on her studies because of her worries about the money.

'Forget about the money. Cicerius will pay me a bundle when I take the prayer mat back. I'll give you your share.'

We find a landus to take us down to Twelve Seas. I ask Makri why she was discussing gambling with Hanama, but her reply is non-committal and I don't pursue it. I'm elated at finally making some progress. Pontifex Derlex. The man who claimed that the Orcs didn't even have a religion. And here he is, reading all about it. Then removing the prayer mat no doubt. It makes sense. The True Church was always a strong candidate for sabotaging the Orcs, and the Pontifex is an ambitious young man. If Bishop Gzekius was casting around for volunteers he'd be first in line.

Derlex lives in a small house in the grounds of the church in Saint Volinius's Street. We march right up and knock on the door. The door swings open. I draw my sword and we advance cautiously. I note that the house is poorly furnished, in contrast to the splendid mansion inhabited by Bishop Gzekius. No lamps are lit in the evening gloom so I take out my illuminated staff and speak the command to give us more light.

A groan comes from somewhere along the corridor. As we arrive in the main room Derlex is struggling to rise from the floor. There's a large candlestick beside him and it looks like he's been clubbed to the ground. I feel his pulse and check his wound.

'You'll live.'

Derlex groans again and struggles to focus his eyes.

'Was this connected with a certain Orcish prayer mat?' I demand.

His hand reaches out to the chair behind him. There's nothing on it. 'It's gone,' he says, and slumps back to the floor.

'Who told you to steal it?' I ask, but Derlex isn't talking any more. He slips back into unconsciousness. I have a quick look round, but don't find anything.

'Too late,' I mutter to Makri. 'At least we're on the trail.'

I send a message to the Bishop informing him that his Pontifex might not be able to take services for a day or two. Then I send another message to Cicerius giving him a full description of events. At least he'll know I'm busy.

'Who do you think took it?' enquires Makri.

'No idea. I'll think about it tomorrow. Right now it's time for food, beer and some celebration.'

After that smart piece of investigating, I figure I'm fully entitled to some relaxation. I head back to the Avenging Axe for a bite to eat, an early beer, and then a nap to prepare me for the full rigours of the night.

By the time midnight rolls around on the last day of the Hot Rainy Season, celebrations are in full swing all over the city, nowhere more so than in the Avenging Axe. Nowhere more so than at my table, actually. Palax and Kaby are perched on the bar playing a flute and a mandolin. They're looking as weird as ever. No one else in Turai has pierced eyebrows and they actually dye their hair bright colours, something I didn't even know was possible till they arrived. Gave me quite a shock when I first saw them. They're leading the revellers in raucous renditions of popular favourites while Gurd, Makri, Tanrose and another couple of bar staff hired specially for the occasion fill flagon after flagon of ale.

The bar is full of singing mercenaries, dancing dockers, drunken fish vendors and smiling labourers. Everyone, including me, forgets their troubles for the night. Outside the rain is still pounding down, but tomorrow the clouds will roll away, the sun will shine and preparations for the Turas and Triple-Moon Conjunction festivals will get under way. I forget all about Mursius, Orcs, prayer mats, death threats and crime in general and concentrate on getting as many giant 'Happy Guildsman' tankards of ale down my throat as is humanly possible.

Kemlath is sitting by my side and he's about as happy as a drunken mercenary. 'I haven't had such a good time since the celebrations after the war,' he tells me. 'I'd forgotten what a good night in a tavern was like.'

A young prostitute sits down on his lap and admires his rainbow cloak and his fine jewellery. Kemlath takes off a bracelet and gives it to her. He's a generous man, the big Sorcerer, and he buys drinks all round, which makes him popular. The only person who doesn't seem to be smiling is Makri. She doesn't have any money and Minarixa the baker is sitting right at the bar, which is embarrassing for her.

'What's the matter with your friend?' asks Kemlath.

I explain to him that Makri has made somewhat of a blunder in gambling away the money she'd collected for the Association of Gentlewomen. Kemlath roars with laughter.

'The Association of Gentlewomen,' he thunders. 'A bunch of harridans. A plague on them!' He laughs some more, and catches Makri as she sways past with a tray of beers on her arm. She frowns.

'Don't frown,' cries Kemlath. He taps his illuminated staff on the floor, causing a rainbow to magically appear in the room. Everyone cheers, but Makri remains unmoved. Kemlath reaches into some corner of his voluminous robe and pulls out a fat purse.

'How much do you owe them?'

'Sixty gurans.'

'A woman like you shouldn't owe sixty gurans,' cries

Kemlath. He says that he hasn't seen such an impressive demonstration of unarmed combat as Makri showed at Mox's shop this evening since he himself knocked three Orcs off the city walls after his spells had run out. Without hesitation the Sorcerer counts out twelve five-guran pieces and hands them to Makri. Makri is too wise to question such a gift. She grabs them, stuffs them in her purse, wriggles her way through the crowd to deliver her tray of beer, then beats a path to Minarixa and her friends at the bar. Through the haze of thazis smoke I see her handing over the money. From Minarixa's reaction and Makri's smile, it seems to do the trick. Makri is back in the good books of the A.G.

She struggles her way back to us.

'Thanks,' she says to Kemlath. 'I'll pay you back.'

'Don't worry about it,' says the Sorcerer.

A flicker of suspicion crosses Makri's face as she wonders exactly what Kemlath might expect in return for his sixty gurans, but he doesn't seem to want anything. He's just carried away by the good time he's having in the Avenging Axe. It can hit you like that, sometimes, when you're only used to the refined and rather dull pleasures of the upper classes.

So now Makri is happy too. In the heat of the tavern, sweat pours down her near-naked figure. Makri has discovered that glistening skin seems to be good for tips and reckons she might as well use it to her advantage. The purse that hangs on a long string round her neck is bulging.

'I was going to give you a hard time for that chariot losing,' she tells me. 'I won't now. But you're still a lousy gambler.'

'Nonsense. Didn't I pick you plenty of winners? No one can do it all the time. Just wait till the Turas Memorial. I'm going to leave that race meeting a wealthy man. The Stadium Superbius has never seen anything like the damage I'm going to inflict on the bookmakers.'

Makri grins. 'Won't you be too busy looking after the Orcs?'

'Don't remind me. They won't even be racing if I don't find that prayer mat. But now I've made a start I expect I'll track it down soon enough. You know me, dogged.'

Gurd takes a break to join Kemlath and me, and we start swapping war stories. The arrival of Lord Rezaz has stirred a lot of memories and we reminisce about this and that till Gurd is called away to change a barrel of beer in the cellar.

A woman falls on top of me. It's Sarija. Her cloak is wet and mud-splattered and she's full of dwa.

'I thought you'd be having a good time in Twelve Seas,' she says, and falls off my lap and on to the floor. Kemlath helps her into a seat.

'Where does a woman get a beer around here?' she demands, banging on the table till Makri arrives.

'Wish I had your figure,' says Sarija. 'But bring me a beer anyway.'

Another wet hand paws at my shoulder. It's Kerk, who's just arrived looking very poorly indeed. He doesn't waste any time but thrusts a small bust of an Elf into my hand.

'From Mursius's collection,' he yells, above the din. 'Found it at Axa's.' Axa is another purveyor of stolen goods who operates around the harbour.

He holds out his hand for payment. His face carries

the haunted look that descends on a man when he needs dwa more than anyone has ever needed anything in the world before. It takes me a few seconds to register. I nod dumbly, and fish in my purse for some gurans, and probably end up paying him too much. He departs without a word. I give the bust a quick glance then stuff it in my bag.

'More evidence?' says Kemlath. 'Do you want me to study it?'

'Tomorrow, ' I reply. 'It can wait.'

Kemlath expresses some surprise at my casual manner. I spread my hands.

'It's okay. You see, Kemlath, criminals in this city aren't really that smart. They always leave some trail behind them. People think I must be doing something pretty dammed clever to keep catching them. That's why I keep up the pretence of Sorcerous Investigator when really I can hardly do any sorcery. Good for the reputation. I like people to think I'm moving heaven, earth and the three moons to put these crooks behind bars. In reality I just plod along the trail till I catch up with them.'

'What if you run up against someone really smart?'

'Hasn't happened yet. More beer?'

The revelry continues all through the night. Kemlath shows me a good trick for conjuring rainbows out of my illuminated staff. I send rainbows all over the tavern, up people's legs and into their drinks, which keeps me entertained. It's years since anyone taught me any new magic. Sarija drinks herself unconscious and falls asleep on Kemlath's lap. I smoke so much thazis I can barely join in with the soldiers' drinking songs initiated by Gurd.

'You're a fine man,' I tell Kemlath, putting my arm
round his shoulder. 'One of the best. These other
Sorcerers are all stuck-up snobs. I hate them. But you,
you're a soldier. I always did like you.'

Makri is happy. She's back in favour with the A.G. and
she's making loads of tips. She swings lithely through
the crowd, dealing out beers to customers and slaps to
anyone whose hands show signs of straying as she
passes, though in quite a friendly way for Makri. No
bones are broken. When she takes another break she
joins us for a while and gets into conversation with
Kemlath, who seems quite taken with her. As the big
Sorcerer is definitely a more cultured man than your
average Twelve Seas drinker, Makri finds him interesting. She tells him about her current projects at the Guild
College and mentions the plants she brought back from
Ferias for her natural history class.

'Strange things,' she says. 'Even my tutor isn't sure
what they are.'

Something nags at me. I try and ignore it. I don't want
things to nag at me when I'm having a good time. I drink
another beer. No good, it's still nagging. Why did
Mursius have rare unknown plants in his window boxes?
No reason, probably. I drink another beer. Again it's no
good. It won't go away. Sometimes I hate these Investigator's intuitions. Won't leave a man alone to enjoy
himself. I drag myself out of my chair and upstairs,
along to Makri's room. This is furnished with extreme
simplicity, as Makri has very few possessions. Nothing
but a cloak, some books and a lot of weapons. In contrast
to me, Makri is very tidy and her few belongings are
neatly positioned around the room.

She's rooted the plants in little pots of earth beside the window. I grab one of them and take it downstairs, fighting my way through the throng to where Chiaraxi the healer and Cospali the herbalist are sitting at a table in the corner. Both women are unusual in that they run shops in Twelve Seas, a rare activity for a woman. Both are, incidentally, supporters of the Association of Gentlewomen, probably because they are not allowed to join the trade Guilds, which is bad for their business.

'Either of you ever see this plant before?'

They study it. Chiaraxi shakes her head but Cospali thinks it might be a variety of the coix plant, which they use in the far west for treating delirium.

'What would its effect be if used on a horse?'

'A sedative, maybe, if it's the same sort of plant.'

I work my way back to Makri and Kemlath. I clap Makri a little too enthusiastically on the shoulder.

'What you trying to do, break my arm?'

'Sorry.'

I brandish the plant. 'You know what this is for?'

'No.'

'Doping horses, that's what it's for. That's why Mursius was so optimistic about his chances in the race. He was planning to dope the other horses.'

Sarija, Mursius's wife, is slumped beside us. I ask her about the plants, but she's too drunk to make any sort of sensible reply. I shake her shoulder. Suddenly Kemlath grabs my arm.

'Don't do that,' he says.

They've been drinking together. Obviously the Sorcerer's manners are better than mine.

He apologises to me for speaking sharply, but points

out that Sarija has been having a hard time and is entitled to some stress-free relaxation. I'm sure he's developed a passion for her.

I trust my intuition. Senator Mursius, war hero of Turai, was about to engage in some very dubious business at the races. I wonder if Sarija knew about it. She's planning to enter Mursius's chariot in the race. Is she still planning to cheat? Right now she is incapable of administering sweets to a child, let alone carrying out a large-scale doping operation, but who knows, the Senator might have engaged others to do the work for him. He might have been working with the Society of Friends, for instance.

I'm too full of beer to think it through. Tomorrow I'll come up with something.

Palax and Kaby work up a furious rhythm loud enough to wake Old King Kiben and the place starts swaying as the drinkers bang their tankards on the tables. I join in heartily and stamp my staff on the floor in time to the music, sending rainbows out in all directions. Tomorrow the rain will end. Everyone is happy.

The last thing I remember is berating the Sorcerers Guild for being too snobbish to let an honest workman like myself be a member, and then criticising the King, the Consul and the Deputy Consul for being too useless to run the city properly. After that it's all a bit of a blur and I fall asleep in my chair with a flagon of ale in one hand and a thazis stick in the other.

CHAPTER FIFTEEN

I wake up in the chair. My back hurts and my neck is stiff. I'm too old to be falling asleep in chairs. Sarija is sleeping on the floor. She's wrapped up in Kemlath's rainbow cloak and the Sorcerer slumbers alongside, his arm draped protectively over her. Various other people are slumped all around. Gurd is usually careful to clear the Avenging Axe at night, but as he himself is unconscious at the bar I guess he didn't have the energy.

I check my bag for the small statue Kerk brought me last night. It's gone.

Dim light filters through the windows. I can hear the rain battering down outside. That's strange. The Hot Rainy Season ended last night.

I struggle to the door. Sure enough, the rain is still pouring down out of a grey sky. In all my years in Turai I can't ever remember this happening before. The seasons might be grim, but they're regular. The effort of moving has made my head hurt. I'm feeling rough. What I need is a lesada leaf. I trudge upstairs to find one.

Makri is creeping along the upstairs landing looking one step ahead of death. She groans as I appear.

'I should never have come to this city. You're all decadent. My head hurts. Got any leaves left?'

I nod. She follows me into my room and I remove a small pouch from my desk. Inside are my twenty or so remaining lesada leaves. I took them from a dead Elf a few months ago. He was killed after trying to cross Hanama. Before making the mistake of thinking he could outwit the Assassins he had been a healer and used the lesada leaves for treating all sorts of maladies. I've found them highly effective against hangovers. Best thing I ever got from an Elf in fact.

Makri struggles to swallow her leaf then sits silently beside me while we wait for them to take effect.

'Have you noticed there's a threat painted on your wall?' she says, after a while.

I hadn't.

Stay away from the Mursius investigation, it says. The message is written in blood. Or a magical imitation of it. I hope it washes off.

Underneath is a letter G. Glixius Dragon Killer, presumably. I wonder why he doesn't just attack, instead of leaving these stupid messages. I tell Makri that the bust of the Elf has disappeared during the night.

'It's my own fault. Never fall asleep from too much beer when you're carrying vital evidence. First thing I learned as an Investigator.'

'You think Glixius sneaked in during the night and stole it?'

'Maybe. He's just the sort of evil character who wouldn't be celebrating like everyone else.'

We lapse back into silence. 'Thank God for these leaves,' says Makri some time later, as the colour returns to her face. 'But you ought to go easy. They're running out.'

'I know. I'll have to mount an expedition to the Southern Islands to get some more.'

The fabulous Southern Islands, home to the Elves, are far, far away, and difficult to reach. You need a well-equipped ship to cross the ocean and the Elves are extremely wary of who they let visit. I went there a long time ago, but very few others in Turai have. The idea of actually going back there just to pick up a hangover cure makes us smile.

'Did you notice it's still raining?'

'Oh no!' wails Makri and hurries to the door. She stares in fury at the rain and starts complaining as if it's my fault.

'You promised it would stop. I can't stand any more rain. What's wrong with this place?'

I'm stuck for an answer. It's never happened before.

The celebratory joy evaporates immediately and the entire city plunges back into depression and anxiety. The continuing rainfall is regarded as the gravest of omens. No one has to look far for the cause.

'It's the Orcs!' thunders Bishop Gzekius.

Bishop Gzekius is standing in for his subordinate, Derlex, who'll be absent from the pulpit for a while.

'The rains shall wash us away!'

It's a powerful sermon from the Bishop, much more passionate than you'd normally hear in Saint Volinius's Church, I imagine, though I'm not really one to judge. I never attend church and have only come today to ask Bishop Gzekius what exactly he thinks he's doing, organising the theft of the Orcish charioteer's prayer mat.

It's an unsatisfactory interview. The Bishop refuses to acknowledge any part in the theft of the prayer mat.

'It is ridiculous to think that Pontifex Derlex could
have spirited away the prayer mat from a villa which was
heavily guarded.'

'You have influence all over the city, Bishop. Enough
to make a few Guards turn a blind eye if necessary.'

Gzekius denies it. He claims to have no knowledge of
Orcish religion and when I tell him that Pontifex Derlex
has been reading up on it in the Imperial Library he says
it is none of his business what his young Pontifexes get
up to in their spare time.

I ask Gzekius who slugged Derlex and made off with
the mat, but again the Bishop is saying nothing. I can't
tell if he organised the sabotage of the Orcs as part of
some wider politicking or simply for reasons of faith.
Sometimes members of the True Church have surprised
me by acting from the sincerity of their beliefs. Not often
though.

Either way, the Bishop doesn't know where the prayer
mat is now. He says that if I pursue the matter he will see
that charges are brought against me for burgling
Derlex's house. I tell him that if he wants to start threatening me he'll have to wait his place in the queue.

'You do seem to be in considerable trouble these days,'
agrees the Bishop, maliciously. He hands me a copy of
*The Renowned and Truthful Chronicle of All the World's
Events*. It devotes one full side of its single sheet to the
shocking continuation of the rain, joining in with the
general cry that the arrival of Lord Rezaz and his cursed
chariot is to blame. *Only the True Church speaks up for the
people*, it says, and compliments the staunchness of our
local Bishop. Nice publicity for Gzekius. I flip it over. The
other side is devoted entirely to me, unfortunately.

How can it happen, thunders the *Chronicle*, *that the number one suspect for the murder of the Turanian hero, Senator Mursius, has been employed by the government to protect an official Orcish chariot? Is there no end to the corruption in this city? Surely in any honest civilisation Investigator Thraxas would at this moment be climbing the steps to the gallows to receive due payment for his crimes, rather than receiving payment from the King for protecting these foul enemies of humanity. It is bad enough that the Civil Guard, with all the resources of the state behind it, has not yet secured a conviction. Surely it is intolerable in a civilised society that the chief suspect, Thraxas, a man, it must be said, with the most dubious of characters . . .*

And so it goes on. It's a thorough piece. Even I had forgotten about the time I was hauled up in court for stealing a loaf of bread while everyone was engaged in morning prayers. I was very young when it happened and got off with a warning.

'I'd say you were in enough trouble without bothering a Bishop of the True Church,' says Gzekius, summoning a servant to show me out.

Everywhere I go I meet with sullen anger. Even Minarixa seems annoyed when I call in for some provisions, though it could just be the result of the effects of last night's revels. Guardsman Jevox is surprised to see me.

'I was wondering why they let you out of jail. You've been working for Cicerius.'

'That's right. Did you find out anything about the warehouse?'

Jevox hasn't. If he does he'll send me a message.

'You any idea who broke in to the Pontifex's house last night?'

No crime was reported at the Pontifex's. I suppose that was to be expected. It's baffling though. It was hard enough finding one person who'd know enough to steal that prayer mat. How come someone else suddenly knows enough to steal it from Derlex? The entire city can't have been studying Orcish religion. The library only has one scroll.

I walk down to the Mermaid and there Casax the Boss is almost pleased to see me.

'You were right, Investigator. The Society of Friends had infiltrated Twelve Seas. Four of their men were in that warehouse for a week, posing as common labourers.'

Casax isn't sure what they were doing there, though he presumes it was connected with the arrival of the Elvish and Orcish chariots, both of which were stabled temporarily in that very warehouse.

'I figured that myself. And I think I know what they were planning. A doping operation.'

Casax looks sceptical. 'Doping? For the Turas Memorial? No chance, Investigator. The King's Master of Horse inspects every entrant and Melus the Fair checks for doping as well as sorcery. You couldn't get a doped horse past them.'

'Usually you couldn't. But I think the Society came up with something special this time. Namely the coix plant.'

I take out a small fragment of the plant that Makri brought back from Mursius's villa and hand it to him.

'Comes from the far west. Doesn't look anything special, I know. But I've a strong hunch it'll act as a powerful sedative on horses, and it's completely unknown here in Turai. I reckon there's every chance that if the Society managed to feed the correct dose of this to the Orcish and Elvish teams they'd both crawl round the track on the day and neither Melus the Fair nor the Master of Horse would be able to detect a thing.'

Casax stares at the green leaf. 'I'll have it checked out,' he says.

The Brotherhood prefer muscle to magic but they have Sorcerers on call if they need them.

'So, who was behind it?'

I admit I'm not certain but I imagine it must have been Senator Mursius. After all, the plant came from his house.

'And it makes sense. If the Society were planning something like this, who better to work it for them than the man who was entering the strongest Human chariot team? Mursius was very confident about his chances, far too confident for a man who's up against an Elf. I know that Glixius Dragon Killer is involved. He might be the murderer. Maybe they argued over the cut. People like that always do.'

Casax shakes his head sadly. Not even a gangster likes to see a Turanian war hero exposed as a cheat at the races.

'Perhaps he wasn't thinking straight,' I say. 'He had problems with his wife.'

'I hear his wife is entering the chariot anyway. I also hear she likes to soak up dwa. You think she's carrying on the doping operation?'

'I don't know. I doubt it. Anyway, I'll pass some of the leaf on to Melus the Fair. Once she's studied it, it won't get past her.'

Casax smiles. I don't think I've ever seen him do that before. 'Congratulations, Investigator. You seem to have thwarted a Society operation. I like that. I'll tell my men to keep a lookout for Glixius. We'll make sure he doesn't venture down this way again.'

When I leave the Mermaid I reflect that I've never had such a productive meeting with the Brotherhood. Casax might even feel he owes me a favour.

I head off up to the Palace to find Cicerius. The streets down here are impassable for wheeled vehicles and I have to walk a long way up Moon and Stars Boulevard till I find a landus to take me to the Palace. It still looks splendid, despite the deluge, but even here the gardeners are losing the battle with the volume of rain and huge swaths of land lie under water. The numerous officials scurrying around these parts do so with their cloaks pulled tightly round them and their faces downcast, looking no happier than the denizens of Twelve Seas. Cicerius greets me briskly. The Deputy Consul may be the only person in the entire city unaffected by the weather. He gets down to business right away.

'I'm due in the law courts in an hour. I'm defending a Senator on a corruption charge, so I can't spare you much time I'm afraid. Have you found the prayer mat?'

'Almost.'

'Almost is not good enough.'

I relate the full story of Derlex and Gzekius.

Cicerius nods.

'The True Church will have to learn not to meddle in state affairs. Who do you think took the mat from Derlex?'

'I don't have any suspects. It's very strange, Deputy

Consul. Not that people are trying to sabotage the Orcs, we were expecting that. But who else could possibly know of the importance of that mat?'

Cicerius and the Consul are coming under increasing pressure from the King. Cicerius is fair-minded enough to realise that I've been doing my best, but he needs more than that.

'You have to find the mat by tomorrow. If you don't, we lose the copper mines.'

Before I go I tell him a few details of the Mursius case. He takes the news about the Senator and the doping attempt calmly.

'Once I would have been shocked. Not any longer. Nothing surprises me in Turai any more.'

Last summer I helped Cicerius when his son had been supplying dwa to Prince Frisen-Akan, the heir to our throne. Cicerius can have no illusions about the state of our nation. Rotten, in a word.

At my request the Deputy Consul asked a clerk to examine the state of Mursius's finances. He was in grave financial trouble. He'd lost a great deal of money speculating and he was hit badly when several ships to which he had joined with others to offer insurance sank last year in a storm. Much of his land was mortgaged and he had more debts than he could hope to meet.

Poor Senator Mursius. The man fights off the Orcs from our city and becomes a hero. Fifteen years on and he's broke and his wife's addicted to dwa. No wonder he tried to cheat at the races.

Cicerius summons his official carriage and we ride down to Truth is Beauty Lane, where the Sorcerers live.

Melus has a large villa here, luxurious enough though not too ostentatious.

Melus is a powerful Sorcerer from a long line of Sorcerers. She came to public prominence when she was appointed to the job at the Stadium, since when she's become a national favourite. Everyone trusts Melus. She's around the same age as me and fought in the last war. All our Sorcerers did, and their Apprentices. She stood beside her father as he was killed by dragon flame, so I don't imagine she's too happy about having to help the Orc Lord either. I tell Melus the Fair about Senator Mursius's plans for cheating in the races and hand her a leaf from the coix plant. She's grateful though she doesn't admit that it would have fooled her.

'I'd have picked up that something was wrong. Easy as bribing a Senator.'

Sorcerers always have a very high opinion of their own sorcery.

'Who do you fancy for the big race?' I ask her.

She laughs. 'I'm not allowed to speculate.'

I inform her of developments, and admit that I don't know where to look next for the prayer mat.

'I take it Rezaz the Butcher isn't pleased?' I say.

'No he is not,' says Lord Rezaz Caseg, stepping into the room.

I look at Melus reproachfully. She might have told me there was an Orc Lord next door. If I'd known he could hear me I'd have used his proper title.

'So, Investigator, you have failed to locate my charioteer's prayer mat?'

'That's right.'

'Then we shall leave the city tomorrow.'

'There is no need to leave,' says Cicerius, calmly. 'You may have complete confidence in Thraxas. He will locate the missing item.'

Cicerius proclaims this with complete conviction, though I know he doesn't believe it. Lord Rezaz looks thoughtful. With everyone on their best behaviour you might think this was a gathering of old friends. Deputy Consul Cicerius, Melus the Fair and Lord Rezaz Caseg, in white toga, rainbow cloak and black cloak respectively, maintain a high level of dignity. It's left to me to spoil it all. I've been having a hard time keeping calm. I manage until Rezaz's attendant, a short, muscular Orc with a sword at each hip, makes a comment to his Lord in Common Orcish.

Very few people in Turai speak any Orcish. Since Makri arrived, mine has become quite fluent. The attendant's remark produces the slightest of smiles from the Lord Caseg. I turn to Cicerius, bristling with anger. 'That's it, I'm leaving. I refuse to work for an Orc who says I'm too fat to find my own feet.'

I let the attendant have a choice insult, also in Orcish, that I've heard Makri use on occasion.

'How dare you say that about my mother,' he says, drawing his sword.

I draw mine. I've had enough of being polite to Orcs. I like this better.

'Please!' cries Cicerius as he tries to get between us. There's a commotion at the door and Lord Lisith-ar-Moh walks in with his Elvish attendants. He stares in surprise at the sight of myself and the Orc facing each other with swords in our hands.

'What is going on?' demands the Elf Lord.

'Have you met the man responsible for seeing that the Orcs are treated fairly?' says Melus.

Everyone looks at me. I still have my sword in my hand. I suddenly feel very conspicuous.

'Well, he started it,' I say.

The Deputy Consul shoots me a glance that speaks volumes. I sheath my weapon. Cicerius explains to Lisith what has been happening.

The Lords exchange formal bows.

'An epic battle, that day at the walls,' says Rezaz. 'I regretted that my allies were foolish enough to allow your ships to land. Had I been overall Commander of our forces, I would not have permitted it.'

The Elf Lord allows this to pass without comment. Both of them, each with great power, are too skilful and experienced to give anything away in terms of emotions. They hate each other, but they're not going to let it show, not here.

'I hear that your Orcish chariot is a fine vehicle,' says Lisith politely.

'It is. My pride and joy, in these days when warriors must seek their diversions elsewhere. I was looking forward to the race.'

They enter into a discussion, but I don't pay much attention. I'm still insulted at the Orc commenting on my weight. So it is that on this momentous occasion, the first in recorded history in which Orcs, Elves and Humans have a discussion without there being a war going on, I spend my time staring glumly out the window at the rain, drinking wine.

I'm interrupted by a loud cough from Cicerius.

'So, are you in agreement?' he says.

I look blank. 'Sorry, I wasn't listening.'

Cicerius restrains his ire. 'It is suggested that Melus, Azgiz and Lothlan will go with you immediately in an effort to find the prayer mat.'

'Azgiz and Lothlan? Who are they?'

A tall young Elf steps forward, bows, and introduces himself as Lothlan.

'My personal swordsman,' says Lord Lisith.

The Orc who insulted me also steps forward.

'Azgiz,' he says. 'Personal swordsman to Lord Rezaz Caseg.'

I turn to Cicerius. 'You want me to wander round the city with an Orc and an Elf in tow, looking for a prayer mat? Forget it.'

'What choice do we have? I appreciate that you came close to locating it. As does Lord Rezaz. Had you not been so occupied with your wine you might have heard him compliment your powers of investigation. But time is running short. Both Melus and Lothlan should be able to sense any Orcish item. And it seems reasonable that Azgiz should accompany you.'

'Hasn't it struck you that we're not exactly going to be inconspicuous? Not much chance of going anywhere discreetly.'

'Melus can discard her rainbow cloak. Azgiz and Lothlan can cover themselves with hoods. No more objections. There isn't time. You must locate the prayer mat before tomorrow morning. Now go.'

And thus it is that I find myself hunting through the city with the Stadium Sorcerer, an Orc and an Elf. Another momentous and historical occasion, I suppose. Orcs and

Elves have never co-operated before. Neither of them looks happy about it.

I tell them that we'll have to call in for Makri. I refuse to accompany these three on my own. God knows what might happen. Also, I want to see Makri's face when I turn up with an Orc in tow. If she kills him on the spot we can always flee the city. At least we'd get out of the rain.

'It's your fault,' I say to the Orc, as we take our leave.

'What is my fault?'

'The rain. You've cursed the city.'

'Orcs are not perturbed by rain.'

'That's because they're stupid,' I say.

It's not much of an insult. With a few beers inside me I'm sure I can come up with something better.

CHAPTER
SIXTEEN

The rain continues. Some areas of Turai are now under three feet of water. Parts of Twelve Seas can only be reached by raft. Whole communities have to be evacuated to higher ground and across the city miserable groups of refugees are huddled in warehouses, sick, wet and hungry. The death toll from accidental drowning is the highest ever recorded and food is now unavailable in many districts.

Everyone is suffering. Even the sophisticated drainage engineered in Thamlin can no longer cope and the gardens of the rich have turned into swampland. Prayers are being said for an end to the deluge. Even I have added my voice to them. If this keeps up, the Turas Memorial Race will be cancelled. The races are due to begin in two days' time but the chariots can't run in this.

We form a strange company as we troop to my office. One large-sized Investigator and three mysterious hooded figures. Melus walks between Lothlan and Azgiz for fear that the natural antipathy between Orcs and Elves may make them forget our mission and start fighting. Lothlan has already intimated that he finds it difficult to walk down the same street as an Orc, and Azgiz has let it be known that personally he'd rather descend to the fiery pits of Orcish hell than co-operate with an Elf. I am now obliged to be on my best behaviour because Melus promised that if I started any trouble she'd ban me from the Stadium Superbius. As we enter my office, Makri is scrabbling under the couch.

'I was just looking for—' she begins.

'Forget it. You're needed.'

'What for?'

'We're looking for the prayer mat. You already know Melus the Fair, I believe. Allow me to introduce Lothlan the Elf and Azgiz the Orc. Don't make a fuss, there isn't time.'

Makri is horrified as the Orc and the Elf draw back their hoods.

'You can't be serious,' she says.

To make matters worse, Azgiz greets her in a friendly manner while Lothlan the Elf regards her with suspicion.

'I saw you fight in the arena,' says the Orc swordsman.

He addresses me. 'She was undefeated. She was regarded as one of the finest gladiators in history.' He bows to her.

Makri doesn't know how to react to this so she falls back on what she knows and hurries to her room to find a few weapons.

Lothlan's Elvish senses detect Makri's background. He looks displeased. 'Orc and Elf and Human?' he says. 'That is meant to be impossible.'

'Yeah, she's a marvel.'

Makri reappears with a fierce scowl, a sword at each hip, an axe at her belt and knives stuck into her waistband and boots. Round her neck she carries a bag of throwing stars.

'What were you doing under my couch?' I enquire as we make our way through the muddy street.

'Needed money.'

'Don't you learn any morals at these ethics classes?'

'Never mind that. What's the idea of bringing Orcs to the Avenging Axe?'

I fill her in on the details.

'It's outrageous. Cicerius better get me into the University,' says Makri. 'Did you see the way that stupid Elf ignored me?'

I nod. 'At least the Orc was polite. He said you were number one gladiator.'

Makri makes a face. She's none too pleased to encounter anyone who saw her fight in the arena. Too much of a reminder of her days as a slave.

We arrive at Saint Volinius's Church.

'I tracked the prayer mat to the pontifex's house.'

'What now?' asks Melus the Fair.

I admit I've no idea.

'Then why did you bring us here?'

'Where else would I bring you? I never claimed to know where the mat is now. It was you and Cicerius who demanded we all troop off and look for it. This is its last known resting place. Now it's up to you.'

Melus turns enquiringly to Lothlan.

'I seem to have misunderstood the role of an Investigator,' says the Elf, dryly. He starts to sniff the air, trying to detect any sign of Orcish artefacts. 'It's no use,' he says, shaking his head. 'I can't sense anything. Too much Orcish smell around here already.' He looks pointedly at Azgiz.

'The stench of Elves fills my nostrils,' retorts the Orc.

'Quiet,' demands Melus the Fair. She concentrates for a long time. The distant sound of thunder reaches our ears. Another storm heading in. 'This way,' she says finally. She sets off towards the harbour.

I trudge along behind with Makri at my side.

'This is the worst thing you've ever got me into, Thraxas.'

I offer my flask of klee. Only Makri accepts. Melus strides through the mud and the rain with the Orc and the Elf on either side, while we tag along behind. I warn Makri that she'd better not lose control and attack Azgiz.

'Melus has threatened to ban me from the Stadium if I step out of line. I'm worried she might mean it. How's a man supposed to concentrate on his betting with all this going on?' I drink some more klee. 'Not that I can concentrate anyway,' I continue, warming to the subject. 'Not with half the people in the city trying to fix the races. It's scandalous. Some things in life should be sacred, beyond interference, and the Turas Memorial is one of them. When I was young no one would've dreamed of tampering with it. I tell you, Makri, things are getting out of hand. If I suspect any cheating I'm going straight to the Consul to tell him what's what. I will demand he calls a special meeting of the Senate.'

Makri is looking at me with something approaching awe. 'I've never heard you get so worked up before.'

'Well, there's some things in life a man has to care about.'

'Beer and chariot racing?'

'That's right. Beer and chariot racing made me what I am today. And I'm proud of it!'

Melus has led us right down to the waterfront, to some

warehouses just west of the harbour. She asks Lothlan if he can sense anything, but he shakes his head. Melus looks around doubtfully.

'I thought I could sense something Orcish. But it was so faint . . . I've lost it.'

The door of the warehouse opens and four large Orc warriors march out.

'How faint did you say the traces were?'

More Orcs start pouring out waving scimitars and axes.

'Good,' says Makri, who couldn't take much more sneaking about in this company. I grope for my sleep spell and realise that I'm not carrying it. I'm still using all my magic to keep my cloak dry. This is a tactical error. A dry corpse is not such a great thing to be. I have to discard my cloak anyway to free my arms for fighting.

Melus the Fair reacts quickly, raising her hand and blasting the Orcs with a spell. The front row falls down but there's a tangible jolt as the spell runs against something and dissipates into the air. The warehouse door opens again and an Orc in a plain black cloak steps out. Around his head is a small black band holding a black jewel in place on his forehead. I haven't seen that for fifteen years. The black band is the mark of an Orcish Sorcerer, and the black jewel denotes mastery of his art. This Orc can bring down city walls. My spell protection charm is about to be severely tested.

The Orcish Sorcerer barks out a spell. The air turns red and I'm thrown backwards, but my protection charm holds. Melus has placed a barrier between us and the Orcish Sorcerer, preventing his magic from harming our party. It doesn't hold back the Orcish warriors though. They charge through the crackling, red-tinged air, and Makri, Lothlan and myself find ourselves in the middle of a desperate battle for survival.

I'm surprised to see Azgiz at our side. Something wrong there, surely. He should be fighting with the Orcs. I'm glad he's not, though the odds are bad enough as it is. He has a sword in each hand, a manner of fighting rare in the west. Makri is a master of this style, though on this occasion she is using a sword and an axe, to deadly effect. Both Lothlan and myself use a sword and a knife. I'd be better off with a shield but it's not the sort of thing you carry around the city. We're hard pressed. We have our backs to the warehouse wall but although we repel the first assailants we're soon in trouble as the Orcs swarm round our flanks.

I parry a sword thrust from an Orc then stick my knife in him. As I do so he lands a painful cut on my shoulder and I'm only saved from going under by Lothlan who brings his sword down on the Orc's arm then kicks him out of the way.

Suddenly there's a flash of light. Melus has used a spell to give us an escape route. Part of the wall caves in behind us, and we flee back into the warehouse. Melus is unable to bring her full power into play because she's already occupied with keeping the Orcish Sorcerer at bay, but she manages to place a stream of fire behind us, giving us enough time to make it to the door at the far side. It opens. More Orcs pour in.

'Isn't this meant to be a Human city?' I snarl.

'The wagons,' yells Lothlan.

In one corner of the warehouse are four or five empty

carriages, waiting to be loaded. We charge over and drag one of them out.

'Look,' cries Azgiz. 'The prayer mat.'

The prayer mat indeed. We've found it, but it doesn't seem likely we're ever going to return it.

With our backs to the corner and the wagon in front of us we at least have some sort of cover against the superior numbers. I ask Melus to send for assistance and she gasps that she has already sorcerously contacted her Apprentice, telling her to bring help. Twenty or so Orcs remain. As they advance Melus releases a powerful attack and an explosion sends five Orcs hurtling into the air. Unfortunately this gives their Sorcerer an opening. Without warning, the wagon we're using as a barricade bursts into flames.

Makri screams an utterly savage war cry and charges out to make her death stand. The flames are licking round us, and there's no choice but to follow her. I see her whirling into the fray, hacking down Orcs left and right, and I plunge after her. Azgiz is at my side and between us we deal with a couple of them, but there are far too many. Azgiz goes down and I find myself desperately trying to protect him. I see Lothlan sliding his sword elegantly into a huge Orcish warrior, but then he too falls under a blow from an axe. Makri leaps to his side and wards off his attackers but then she is sur-rounded. We're still on our feet, but we're seconds from death. I take a blow from a mace and sink to my knees.

At that moment whistles sound and a squadron of the King's soldiers flood into the warehouse followed by Civil Guards. Melus's message to her Apprentice reached its destination. I struggle to my feet.

'Thraxas, are you all right?'

It's Makri, cut and bruised, but still in one piece.

I nod. I notice I smell strongly of klee. 'They broke my flask.'

Both Lothlan and Azgiz are lying on the ground. Melus is kneeling over the Orc, protecting him from the soldiers and Civil Guards who are mopping up. I suddenly feel faint from the blow I received, and sit down heavily next to a wagon. There's something uncomfortable underneath me. I drag it out. It's a small silver statue of a Mermaid, a strange thing to find in a deserted warehouse.

Down on all fours I crawl under the wagon.

'Look, Makri,' I say, emerging with another small statue and a painting. 'I just found the rest of Mursius's stolen artwork.'

'You just can't stop investigating, can you?'

'I know. I amaze myself sometimes.'

'Careful,' says Makri. 'You're bleeding over them.'

She's right. We both are. I shout to Melus. 'How about a little medical attention round here?'

There is a great deal of confusion as the Guards send out patrols in pursuit of the Orcs who escaped, and messages are sent to dignitaries all over the city. Some time later I find myself comfortably seated in a large reception room in Prefect Drinius's official residence in Twelve Seas, drinking wine. I am here as his guest, which makes a change. After our desperate battle we are all heroes. Makri and I are in fairly good shape, having been attended to by both Melus the Fair and Chiaraxi the healer. Lothlan and Azgiz were more seriously wounded and will take a few days to recover fully.

'My superior street-fighting skills,' I tell Captain Rallee, by way of explanation. 'The Elf is not a bad fighter. No doubt in a forest he'd be hard to beat. But when it comes to slugging it out in the slums, I'm number one chariot. Incidentally, what were all the Orcs doing there?'

The Captain doesn't know. 'You're a busy man these days. If you keep up the hero act they might let you off with murdering Senator Mursius.'

'Very funny. I didn't kill him.'

'Then who did?'

'Glixius Dragon Killer.'

'Have you got any evidence?'

I shake my head. 'But I'll find it. He's not getting away from me this time.'

Drinius's residence is full of senior Guard Captains, Army officers, Sorcerers from the Palace and various other important city officials. The mysterious appearance of so many Orcs in the city has stirred the government into action. As I'm talking to Captain Rallee, the Consul and the Deputy Consul arrive. Cicerius acknowledges me but immediately goes into conference with Melus the Fair and Old Hasius the Brilliant.

The Captain doesn't know what the Orcs were doing there. I guess I'll find out soon enough. I summon a servant and ask him for some beer. He tells me there is none and offers me some wine.

'I need beer. Send out for some. Remember, I just saved you from a load of Orcs.'

Lord Lisith-ar-Moh walks majestically into the room, flanked by his tall Elvish attendants. He walks right past the Consul and comes over to Makri and me.

'Lothlan has told me of the battle,' he says to us. 'I understand that you stood over him when he fell. He would certainly have been killed had it not been for you. He has asked me to thank you, which I now do. And you have my personal thanks as well.'

He bows lightly to me, and then, with the sort of courteous gesture you find among important Elves, he takes Makri's hand and kisses it. She gapes at him in surprise and stammers out a thank you. Lisith walks off to confer with Kalius and Cicerius, leaving me and Makri with our social status greatly improved. Not everyone in this city gets personally thanked by an Elf Lord. Everyone looks impressed.

A young Elf, who may be the one that stared in surprise at Makri when the ship was being unloaded, also walks over to thank us. His salutation to me is brief and formal. I suspect the real reason is that he has suddenly had a desire to kiss Makri's hand as well, which he does, though formal Elvish etiquette doesn't absolutely demand it. Makri blushes. I've never see her do that before. The Elf hopes he'll see her at the Turas Memorial, then departs after his Lord.

Makri is left confused, unused to having her hand kissed by Elves.

'You're blushing.'

'What?'

'Blushing.'

Makri claims not to know what the word means. I explain it. 'That's the most stupid thing I've ever heard,' she says. 'I don't believe it happens.'

A tall figure swathed in a black cloak arrives in the

now crowded reception room. Even among the city's important figures few have been introduced to Lord Rezaz Caseg and there is a frisson of shock as he draws back his hood. Many of these government officials, Army commanders and Sorcerers were young soldiers themselves the last time Rezaz the Butcher was here and they're reliving similar memories to the ones which have flooded my own mind recently. Consul Kalius prepares to greet him but the Orc walks right over to me.

'Azgiz wishes me to thank you for saving his life,' says the Orc Lord.

'Think nothing of it,' I reply.

He turns to Makri and thanks her. I dig down into my bag and bring out the prayer mat.

'Tell your charioteer I was as careful with it as I could be.'

Lord Rezaz's eyes light up. He takes the prayer mat with every sign of pleasure, and then holds out his hands in a gesture that encompasses both myself and Makri.

'This is excellent! Now the race can go ahead. I am indebted to you both. I proclaim you friends of the Orcish nation of Soraz!'

He walks off with the mat in his hands, talking animatedly with his attendants. I notice that everyone seems to be looking at me. I'm not sure if my social status just went up or down. A friend of the Orc nations is not necessarily such a good thing to be.

'I can't take much more of this,' says Makri. 'Did that servant bring you any beer? Pass it over.' She downs a large gulp from my goblet. 'What were the Orcs doing there anyway?'

No one has provided an official explanation as yet, but I'm fairly sure I know.

'I think they were agents of Prince Kalazar, Rezaz's rival for the throne of Soraz. They were here to kill Lord Rezaz. We just helped save the life of an Orcish monarch. You ought to be proud, Makri. I know I am.'

'Is that a joke?'

'Yes.'

We depart. It's still raining.

'Will the races go ahead now?' asks Makri.

'Not if this doesn't stop.'

Makri is perturbed. 'Stupid place to build a city, ' she says, not for the first time.

CHAPTER
SEVENTEEN

I wake up early. It's the day of the Turas Memorial Race. The rain is still beating down. For the first time ever, the race looks like it might be cancelled.

A faint tap comes at my door. It's Casax, with a huge cape protecting him from the elements. It's unusual for the Brotherhood Boss to go anywhere without a few strong-arm men to protect him. Normally such a visit would be cause for concern but right now we seem to be co-operating.

'I thought I'd fill you in on a few details, Investigator. This is private. As far as anyone else is concerned, you heard nothing from me.'

I nod.

'I found out some more from Axilan, this guy we picked up last night, who was trying to sell us some information. You were right about the warehouse. The Society of Friends was using it. They had men hiding there, waiting to drug the Elvish horses with that coix plant from the far west. But it seems they were taken by surprise when they were offered some works of art for sale.'

'You mean Mursius's art?'

'That's right.' Casax glances at the pile of artefacts in the corner. 'I see you've recovered the junk.'

'Some of it's quite valuable.'

'I never was an art lover. According to Axilan they were hiding out when suddenly this Sorcerer appeared.'

'What Sorcerer? Glixius?'

'That's right. And he tells them to use their contacts to sell the goods. They were surprised, but they knew Glixius was well connected to the Society of Friends and was part of the doping operation. So they dumped the stuff upstairs, planning to remove it when it was all over. They couldn't work out why Glixius didn't dispose of the goods in the north of the city, where he had plenty of contacts, but he was too scary to argue with. Anyway, it was valuable stuff and they stood to make a good profit.

'So Axilan carries on waiting for the Elves to arrive when one day he hears a terrible argument upstairs, which surprises him as he didn't know there was anyone up there. He goes upstairs afterwards and finds Senator Mursius dead. I figure the story is true so far, because he says he saw you come into the warehouse, which you did around that time.'

'What happened next?'

'The Society men panicked. They didn't want to be found in the warehouse with Mursius dead upstairs, so they grabbed a few valuables and ran. They sold them as soon as they could to raise a stake to get out of the city. They didn't want to go back north after bungling the operation. That's why you found a few pieces in the local shops.'

I tell Casax that the goods they left behind were later removed by sorcery. 'I found them in another warehouse close by.'

'I heard,' says Casax. 'When you were being a hero, fighting Orcs. Were they in on the theft?'

'No. Just a coincidence that the rest of the art ended up there. It was the nearest empty warehouse.'

I ask if I can speak to Axilan. Casax shakes his head. 'He doesn't seem to be around any more.'

'You mean he's floating in the harbour?'

'No idea. But he did say he wanted to leave the city quickly.'

I thank Casax for the information.

'No racing in this rain. Must be bad for your business.'

Casax shrugs. 'If people aren't gambling at the Stadium they'll be drinking in our taverns or visiting our whores.'

He departs. I light another thazis stick, and think about Glixius. How did he get hold of Mursius's belongings? I wonder if Sarija sold them directly to him. She used to be a dancer at the Mermaid. Who knows what contacts she might still have in the city. But why did Glixius take them to the warehouse in Twelve Seas? There must have been plenty of other places where he could have disposed of them. It doesn't make much sense. But it does more or less confirm that he killed Mursius.

Glixius Dragon Killer. He's been sending me death threats, interfering with the races, stealing valuables, and murdering a Turanian hero. And putting my aura on the knife that did it, if I'm not mistaken. The man is a plague. I resolve that he is not going to get away with it. I'll see Glixius in court if it's the last thing I do.

The prospect of no race meeting robs me of my appetite for breakfast. I drag out a bottle of beer and drink it while staring gloomily out at the rain. Makri arrives in my room.

'How's life?' she asks.

'Better than rowing a slave galley. No, I take that back. It isn't.'

'Can't the chariots run in the rain?'

'Not if the track's waterlogged.'

Makri scowls. She was looking forward to the races, even if she has no money to gamble with. I told her to keep a little back from the money she promised the A.G. but she wouldn't.

'I can't do that. It's stealing.'

'What about burrowing under my couch looking for my emergency reserve?'

'That's different.'

A carriage pulls up outside and the Deputy Consul alights to wade through the mud. He walks in with his toga still gleaming white, if somewhat damp.

'Important news,' he says.

'The races are on?'

Cicerius shakes his head. 'No. It is unfortunate. It does rather negate the effort we put in to ensuring that the Orcish chariot could compete. Lord Rezaz has no complaint against us however, and the agreement will be honoured. The King is very pleased, Thraxas, and the government fully appreciates the part you played in the recovery of the prayer mat.'

He turns to Makri and thanks her as well. He seems surprised that neither of us leaps around with glee. He notices the collection of fine art I now have dumped in a corner.

'Belonging to the late Senator Mursius? Have you found the killer yet?'

'I'm close. Though I guess I'm still the Guard's main suspect.'

'The Guard doesn't really suspect you, Thraxas,' says Cicerius.

'They give a good impression of it. Or was that just to put pressure on me so I'd agree to protect the Orcs?'

'I wouldn't say that,' replies Cicerius. 'After all, there is evidence against you. Your aura really was on the knife, and that circumstance has still to be explained. But I doubt if charges would have been brought.'

He takes out a purse and hands it to me. Reward for services to the city.

'Enough for a few good bets,' I say. 'If there was anything to bet on. Was I right about the Orcs being in the pay of Prince Kalazar?'

'You were. They were transported here by his chief Sorcerer, Makeza the Thunderer, for the purpose of assassinating Lord Rezaz. It was a clever plot. Lord Rezaz's security in his homeland was too thorough to allow his assassination, but there seemed every likelihood that it could be achieved in Turai where he would have only a few attendants with him. Furthermore, while our own Sorcerers would normally detect the arrival of any Orcs in the west, Makeza the Thunderer was able to disguise the presence of Kalazar's Orcs by mixing their aura with that of Rezaz and his attendants. Makeza is a dangerous opponent.'

'Did the Guards pick him up at the warehouse?'

'No, he was long gone by then. Back to the safety of the Wastelands, I imagine.'

'Why did the Orcs steal the prayer mat from Pontifex Derlex?' enquires Makri.

The Deputy Consul smiles. 'To return it, strangely enough. Their assassination was planned for the Stadium Superbius. It was vital for them that Lord Rezaz did not leave the city before it occurred. Makeza the Thunderer learned of its theft through his sorcerous probing, then located it and sent his Orcs to recover it. Pontifex Derlex can count himself extremely fortunate to be alive. The Orcs planned to return it anonymously. Then they would mingle with Rezaz's entourage and murder him on the way to the Stadium.'

'Is there no chance of the race meeting going ahead?' I ask.

Cicerius looks irritated. 'I am told that it cannot go ahead in these conditions. But surely that is of only marginal importance. I never cared much for chariot racing myself,' he says.

'You should take it up,' I tell him. 'Give your image a boost in time for the next election.'

Cicerius is not the sort of man to give his image a boost in this manner. He relies on honesty and integrity. He'll never make Consul. Outside his driver is having problems. The carriage is stuck in the mud. Thus it is that I find myself out in the rain trying to pull Cicerius's official carriage free while the local street vendors look on with amusement. The combined force of two horses, two attendants, two Guards, Makri and myself fails to budge it.

'Can't we just leave him?' says Makri.

'Not if you want Professor Toarius to pass your work at college.'

It's useless. The carriage won't move. Cicerius himself gets out and lends a hand, making a fairly amusing sight in his white toga. Its green edges are soon coated in filth. While we're pushing, the call for morning prayers, Sabam, sounds around the city. I'm appalled. How could I be so careless? Makri lets out a despairing groan.

'I'm already as wet as a Mermaid's blanket. You expect me to kneel down in this?'

With Guards, attendants and the Deputy Consul right beside us, there is no escaping it. Even the Deputy Consul, a pious man, does not look particularly pleased to kneel down in the mud and the rain to pray. I whisper to Makri to stop grumbling.

'Pray for the rain to stop and we might get to the races.'

I send up a devoted prayer while sinking into the swamp. By the time the call for the end of prayers sounds I'm embedded about a foot deep and have some difficulty extracting myself. I'm covered in mud. With the mess, the rain, and the prospect of a cancelled race meeting, I am about as miserable as a Niojan whore and see no possibility of things improving.

'The rain's stopped,' says one of Cicerius's attendants.

We all look up. It's true. The rain has stopped. Furthermore, blue sky is visible on the horizon.

'The rain has stopped!'

I practically dance for joy as the sun begins to shine. Word spreads and happy people start to appear on the streets.

Kemlath Orc Slayer appears from the tavern.

'Having some trouble?' he says, seeing Cicerius's plight. He makes a motion with his hand and a little jolt runs through the carriage. The horses whinny and suddenly it's free.

'Nice spell, Kemlath. Pity you didn't get here earlier.'

I accost the Deputy Consul before he drives off. 'How's the drainage system at the Stadium? Well maintained?'

'Certainly,' he replies. 'I allocated the budget myself. And I'll send over extra men to clear up.'

'You think the race meeting will start on time?'

'It will,' says Cicerius, whose political reputation might now take a knock if it doesn't.

We tell Gurd and Tanrose the good news.

'I said a prayer and the rain stopped,' says Makri.

There's bustle and excitement as everyone prepares to travel up to the Stadium Superbius. Gurd will shut the tavern for the day and come along with Tanrose. Palax and Kaby are planning to busk to the crowds, and maybe place a few bets if they earn enough. Myself and Makri are in reasonable shape after the reward money from Cicerius. He gave me sixty gurans. I extract ten to repair the damage to my rooms inflicted by various sorcerous warning messages and such like, and split the rest with Makri, which gives her twenty-five gurans. I have fifty, which puzzles Makri.

'Where did you get the extra twenty-five?' she asks suspiciously.

'I pawned my illuminated staff. Still not much of a stake, but I'll soon build it up. Follow me, and you won't go wrong. I'm going to make these bookmakers wish they'd joined the Army.'

Makri wonders if anyone will try to sabotage the Orcish chariot again.

'I doubt it. It's too late. The Consul has Guards everywhere and Old Hasius the Brilliant is watching out in case the Thunderer shows his face again.'

For the first time in a month I don't bother putting the dry spell on my cloak. Instead I use my magical capacity to load up with the sleep spell. I'm not expecting any more trouble but it's best to be prepared. I'm in a notably good mood.

'It's amazing how the prospect of gambling cheers you up, Thraxas. Only yesterday you were complaining that everything was a disaster. You said your reputation was in shreds because everyone was calling you an Orc friend and what's more you hadn't found Mursius's killer.'

I wave this away. 'Minor problems, Makri. I found the artwork, didn't I? I'll track down the killer soon enough. If some high-class Sorcerer at the Abode of Justice can find a link between the stolen goods and Glixius it'll be enough to take him to court. If not, I'll just have to do a little more leg work. Either way, I'll sort it out after the races.'

Kemlath Orc Slayer compliments me on my perseverance. 'You're right, Thraxas, you are a hard man to shake off. Glixius should have known better than to tangle with you.'

Kemlath is travelling with us up to the Stadium, where he's planing to meet Sarija and lend her support for the chariot she's entering in the big race.

Mursius's stuff is still in my room: fancy cups, statues, and the painting of him as a young man after the Orc wars.

'How come you weren't in the painting?' asks Makri.

'I was a common soldier. They only painted the officers and Sorcerers.'

'It's a lousy painting,' says Makri, who, along with

everything else, is now an art critic. I wouldn't know. At least you can recognise the people in it. I always think a painting can't be that bad if you can recognise the people. It was this item which Mursius particularly wanted to recover. I stare at it. Mursius, Kemlath, a few other officers I recall. I have memories of the war again, but banish them, and we continue with the business of the day. Tanrose is bustling about merrily, packing food for the trip.

'I really thought the race would be cancelled.'

'I just said a prayer and the rain stopped,' says Makri.

I have a bag of thazis sticks, a few beers and fifty gurans. It's time to go racing.

CHAPTER
EIGHTEEN

The Stadium Superbius is an enormous stone amphitheatre built by King Varquius a hundred years ago. It's the setting for circuses, theatrical performances, religious ceremonies, gladiatorial shows and, best of all, the chariot races. During the racing season the amphitheatre is packed full of racegoers from every stratum of Turanian society. Praetors, Prefects, Senators, priests, society ladies, Sorcerers and high-ranking Guild officials all mingle with the huge mass of proletarian Turanians out to enjoy themselves for the day, and maybe pick up a little money on the side. Today, for the Turas Memorial Race, the place will be bursting at the seams.

The gloom that has recently enveloped the city disappears with the rain. Being able to walk around without getting wet is enough to make most people cheerful and the prospect of the race definitely taking place brings a smile to the faces of even those who only yesterday were confidently predicting that we were all cursed by the gods. The relief is so great that anger about the Orcs is largely replaced with anticipation to see the race between them and the Elves. The Elf is a strong favourite. Few Turanians will bet money on the Orcs, even if some do suspect that they might have a chance of victory. Sarija has entered Storm the Citadel, and although I personally think it has no chance of winning it's the best of the Human entrants and will also gather a large amount of popular support.

Entering the Stadium is tough. I have to use my weight to force my way through, with Makri bringing up the rear.

'I admit your bulk does have some advantages,' she says, as I forcefully negotiate a path for us through a large group of schoolchildren who are far too tardy in finding their seats. We settle down in a good position near to the track, with easy access to both the book-makers and a beer tent. All Turai is here. Tumblers and jugglers cavort before the crowds. The great mass of the people sits in the huge banks of terraces that run round the banks of the Stadium, and the Senators and other important people are up in the reserved galleries. I catch sight of a few green Elvish hoods up there and possibly a black Orcish one well back from public view.

Right at the front of this gallery, very visible to the public, is Melus the Fair in her rainbow cloak. The sight gives everyone confidence. Melus the Fair, bless her name, will protect us gamblers from unwanted outside interference.

I have fifty gurans. Makri has twenty-five. I'm surprised that the normally cautious Makri has brought all her money with her. I would've expected her to put some aside for necessities.

'I'm feeling confident,' she says. 'I think I have the hang of this now.'

Makri is happy. Here in the Stadium everyone is too busy with the racing to bother about minor distractions such as a young woman with one-quarter Orc blood wearing a man's tunic and carrying two swords. At times like this such things fade into insignificance. The whole place is still damp and steam rises in the midday heat, but the track is in reasonable condition. It is wide enough to allow eight chariots to run at once, which makes for an exciting spectacle. We settle down with some beers.

'I'm feeling sharp as an Elf's ear today,' I say, and get down to studying the form sheet.

The favourite is Glorious North Wind at six to five on.

'Glorious North Wind for the first race. Certain winner.'

'I don't fancy it,' replies Makri, surprising me. 'I like the look of Eastern Beauty.'

Eastern Beauty is the close second favourite in the race, quoted at evens by the bookmakers. It's not a bad bet, actually, though I prefer the favourite. When I ask Makri why she prefers Eastern Beauty she says she likes the name.

'You can't just bet on a chariot because you like the name.'

Makri won't be swayed. Obviously she wishes to demonstrate that she can make up her own mind and, as I say, Eastern Beauty isn't such a bad prospect. There's nothing else in the race worth backing. None of the other chariots are fancied any better than sixteen to one and I'm in no mood for incautious speculation. Honest Mox has set up a stall in the stadium, manned by his son, and we make our way over to place our bets. I bet five of my fifty and Makri bets four of her twenty-five, then we settle down in the sunshine to watch.

After a fanfare of trumpets and a speech from the Consul the chariots make their way out from the stables. It's one of my favourite sights. Eight chariots, eight riders, thirty-two horses, poised to do four laps of the track. Terrific.

The starter drops a flag, the chariots set off, and the crowd erupts with a mighty roar. Glorious North Wind takes an early lead and by the end of the first lap is in a commanding position. The charioteers flog the beasts mercilessly as they thunder around the track. There's an early collision as three chariots get tangled up in each other's wheels and crash out of the race. A team of amphitheatre officials rushes on to clear the wreckage before the others come round again.

At the end of the third lap Glorious North Wind has a substantial lead with the other four disputing second place. Eastern Beauty, Makri's choice, is not making much of a showing. I'm on my feet along with everyone else, screaming encouragement at the favourite.

I have often thought that the gods are displeased with me. Perhaps it's the way I keep missing prayers. With half a lap to go and a clear run to the finish, Glorious North Wind loses a wheel and skids to a messy halt in the centre of the track. Three of the pursuing chariots crash into the wreckage, spilling their unfortunate charioteers heavily on to the ground. Eastern Beauty, currently in last place, swerves to avoid the pile-up and trots home an easy winner. There's a great groan from the crowd. Makri is still on her feet, however, shouting and yelling, and she practically tramples her neighbours to death in her eagerness to collect her winnings. She arrives back brandishing a fist full of coins.

'I won four gurans!'

I manage a grin. I'm not very pleased but I can't begrudge my companion a bit of good fortune, so long as it doesn't happen too often.

'What're you betting on next, Thraxas?'

I study the sheet. 'Dragon's Breath,' I announce finally.

Makri makes a face. 'Don't like the sound of that. I'm going for Lilac Paradise.'

'Lilac Paradise? What sort of a name is that for a chariot?'

'I like it,' insists Makri.

'It's got no form whatsoever.'

I stare suspiciously at my companion. This seems like a very rash bet by Makri's standards. Lilac Paradise is a rank outsider at twenty to one. It's one of the chariots owned by Magadis, a very rich aristocratic widow. She's a racing enthusiast and has been training chariots for years, but she's not one of our more successful racers. Lilac Paradise is a poor chariot, even by her standards.

'I still like it,' says Makri.

'Five gurans on Lilac Paradise,' says Makri, handing over her money to Mox's son

Dragon's Breath is second favourite at three to one. I place a modest three gurans on it, which is just as well because on the first corner the chariot is involved in an ugly collision and crashes out of the race. Several more collisions follow and to the amazement of the crowd Lilac Paradise wins by half a lap.

There is a great deal of grumbling in the crowd, much of it from me.

'How is a man meant to make a bet when the wheels

fall off his chariot at the first corner?' I complain, and stand up to hurl abuse at the charioteer as he is carried off on a stretcher.

'Orc lover!' I yell. 'Who told you you could ride a chariot?'

My fifty gurans has now shrunk to forty-two. Makri, having picked up an astonishing hundred gurans on Lilac Paradise, now has one hundred and twenty-nine. Rarely have I seen a bookmaker so unwilling to hand over one hundred gurans.

The owner of Dragon's Breath appears on the track, supervising the removal of his mangled chariot.

'Come over here and I'll mangle you as well!' I scream at him.

'Cheating dog!' roars a woman behind me, brandishing a tankard. She has to be restrained by her companions from invading the arena and assaulting the owner.

'The population of Turai doesn't like losing,' observes Makri.

'Damn right we don't,' I grunt.

I'm in no mood for Makri's philosophical observations. I muscle my way to the beer stall and buy a drink. I don't get one for Makri. She's just won a hundred gurans. She can buy her own.

'I like it here,' says Makri, as I return. 'Who do you fancy in the next race?'

The sun beats down. The Stadium is now as hot as Orcish hell and the crowd are restive. What we need here is a popular favourite romping home an easy winner, not a load of outsiders carrying off the prizes. The woman behind me is particularly virulent. I nod in agreement as she roundly lambasts the chariot owners for carving it all up among themselves, cheating the honest punters out of their hard-earned money. I think I recognise her from Twelve Seas and I chat with her about the iniquities of chariot owners while we wait for the next race to get under way.

I note with relief that Warrior Chief, one of the finest chariots in Turai, is due to run. Okay, he's odds-on favourite and I'm not going to win much, but it'll get me back on course. Warrior Chief is an absolute certainty. I back him with twenty gurans at two to one on.

Makri plumps for Serenity of Love, a useless wreck of a chariot pulled by four crippled old horses and ridden by a man who last won a race some time during the Orc Wars. It's another of Magadis's chariots and is something of a joke. The bookies are offering sixteen to one and there are few takers even at that price, apart from Makri. She says she likes the name, and backs it to the tune of thirty gurans.

'You're throwing your money away. Serenity of Love wouldn't win a chariot race if all the other chariots were eaten by a dragon.'

When Warrior Chief fails to complete the race and Serenity of Love strolls in an easy winner I'm not the only one up on my feet baying my disapproval.

'Cheats! Fix!' cries the crowd, along with other things much ruder. Fists are waved angrily and cushions and ripped-up form sheets cascade on to the track. The Civil Guards on duty stand up and face the crowd, nervous about the possibility of a riot. There is massive discontent. The stadium is packed full of punters all seeing their hard-earned cash going down the drain as one unlikely chariot after another comes home a winner. I've rarely seen a race crowd look so ugly. It's fortunate that Melus the Fair has such an impregnable reputation for incorruptibility, else there would be great suspicion that magic was involved. Even so, mistrustful glances are cast in her direction and some slanderous accusations are muttered by the more degenerate members of the lower classes, like myself, for instance.

'Damn that Melus, someone's been bribing her.'

'Nonsense,' replies Makri, cheerfully. 'You said yourself she got the job because of her honesty.'

'Well, you can't tell me that wheel fell off by accident. Even the Sorcerers up in the royal box looked surprised.'

'You're a poor loser, Thraxas.'

'You're damn right I am.'

Makri is now rolling in money, having picked up an astounding four hundred and eighty gurans on Serenity of Love.

'I have six hundred and nine gurans,' she says.

'I don't remember asking you for an exact count.'

I'm now down to twenty-two and facing the prospect of having nothing left for the final race. I remember that Makri owes me fifty – forty for her exam fees and ten that I lent her for betting.

'Hand it over,' I demand.

Makri repays me the fifty gurans with a bright smile, which puts me in a even worse mood. There are a couple of races to go before the big Turas Memorial and the trumpets sound for a break in the proceedings. Makri asks if I want to go with her to find something to eat, but I am in too bad a mood to accompany her.

'I prefer to take luncheon on my own,' I say.

I'm furious about the day's events. There's something strange going on here and I'm going to move heaven, earth and the three moons to get to the bottom of it. Leaving Makri to gloat over her winnings, I depart in the direction of the nearest food vendor.

I'm musing over a large meat pie – one of the Superbius Specials – when I run into the woman from the seat behind me.

'I haven't seen such injustice since they cancelled the races during the Orc Wars,' she says.

I recognise her now. She was the landlady at the Mermaid tavern back in those days. She served me many a drink when I was a thirsty young soldier. She tells me that she married a man with a good position in the Barrel-Makers Guild and moved up to Pashish.

'How's the barrel-making business?'

'Good. It'll have to be, after the amount I've dropped here today.'

I wander away, going nowhere in particular. With the money that Makri repaid me I still have seventy-two gurans, but my confidence has been badly shaken. Near the Senators' boxes I meet Kemlath Orc Slayer. He's on his way down to the owners' enclosure to wish good luck to Sarija, whose chariot will be competing soon.

'I don't suppose she has much chance against the Orcs and Elves,' he says, truthfully. 'But you have to admire her for making the effort. She's a fine woman, Sarija.'

'I noticed you were getting to like her.'

I complain to Kemlath about my bad luck so far.

'You haven't noticed any sorcery being used I don't suppose?'

'Sorcery?' says Kemlath. 'Certainly not. You know Melus wouldn't allow it.'

'I suppose not.'

'Incidentally,' says Kemlath. 'I noticed Glixius Dragon Killer back there.'

He waves his hand, indicating a throng of people. His large ring glints in the sunlight.

'Glixius Dragon Killer. Really?'

I'm reminded of the longstanding rumours about the Society of Friends and their purported betting coup at the races. Could these strange events be the result of that? Have the Society somehow been manipulating things in their favour? I decide to nose around.

Kemlath warns me to be careful, reminding me of Glixius Dragon Killer's sorcerous power.

'To hell with his sorcerous power. I'll make him wish he took up basket-weaving instead.'

I spot quite a few Sorcerers in their rainbow cloaks around the stadium but Glixius's size makes him easily visible. I wade through the crowd towards him. When I reach him he has his back to me and is talking to a Senator.

'I can't understand it,' he's saying. 'Warrior Chief should have won. It was obviously the best chariot in the race. I'm down two hundred gurans today.'

The Senator nods in sympathy; obviously he's suffered heavy losses himself.

'Don't give me that,' I snarl, grabbing Glixius's shoulder. 'You and your Society friends are behind all this.'

He whirls round, a look of contempt and fury on his face. 'Must you harass me everywhere I go?' demands the Sorcerer. 'Were we not in the stadium where sorcery is forbidden I would tear your heart from your chest and jump on it.'

I repeat my accusation. The Senator looks interested. Glixius notices this and he becomes defensive.

'You accuse me of fixing the races? Me? How dare you. I personally have suffered grievous losses.'

'So? You could pretend to do that to throw suspicion off yourself.'

Even as I'm saying this, I'm not entirely convinced. I have long, long experience of gamblers and their reactions to adversity. I hate to admit it, but Glixius Dragon Killer sounds more like a man genuinely aggrieved at his bad luck than a man who's behind it all.

'Do you have any evidence for these accusations?' demands the Senator.

Do I? Not really. Glixius and the Society of Friends were certainly planning some doping, but I can't prove it. I don't even know if the operation carried on after they were interrupted by Mursius getting killed, or if it was cancelled. When it comes right down to it, I have no firm evidence against Glixius, and I don't want to show my hand to him before I do. If I'm going to prove he killed Mursius I shouldn't be giving him advance warning of what I already know. It was rash of me to approach him. My emotions got the better of me.

'Anyone making such accusations without good grounds faces severe penalties in the courts,' says the Senator

I turn on my heel and march away, annoyed with myself. So far today, nothing is going very well.

I find myself next to the Senators' enclosure, which is protected by a low wall. Inside, Melus the Fair is in conversation with Cicerius. I walk up and demand admittance. The Deputy Consul nods to the attendant to let me in.

I march up to the pair of them. Cicerius looks glad to see me.

'I'm pleased you're taking your work seriously,' he says.

'What work?'

'Looking out for sabotage of the Orcish chariot, of course.'

'Sabotage of the Orcish chariot? Sabotage of me, more like.' I turn to Melus the Fair. 'What is going on here? Are you trying to tell me that Serenity of Love won that last race without magical help?'

As I say this, various Senators and Praetors nod their heads in sympathy. It's not only the poor who are suffering in the great gambling disaster that's unfolding here.

Melus smiles. 'It has been a string of unexpected results, I grant you, Thraxas. But I have been monitoring everything very carefully. I can assure you that no sorcery has been used in the stadium. Nor has there been any attempt at doping.'

The Senators all around sigh. It looks like we're all just stuck with our losses.

I'm flummoxed. If Melus says it, then it's true. Besides, there are plenty of other Sorcerers here as spectators. They all specialise in different types of sorcery but surely one of them would notice if anything odd had been happening. I decide to go down to the chariot pen underground and see if I can find out anything there. Maybe someone has been sawing through a few axles.

Cicerius draws me aside as I make to leave. 'You are still in the employ of the city,' he hisses severely. 'Rather than wasting time gambling, I expect you to keep a vigilant lookout for the welfare of the Orcs.'

'To hell with the Orcs,' I hiss back. 'I've more important things on my mind right now.'

I storm off, having again caused my status to plummet in government circles. To hell with them all. I grab a beer and start shoving my way through the crowd again. It's too hot. I wish I hadn't broken my flask of klee. A blind beggar gets in my way. I push him to one side and he falls to the ground, protesting angrily. I ignore him. He was probably putting it on anyway. These beggars, you can never trust them.

At the foot of the terraces there's another row of bookmakers' stalls. People stand in line waiting to place bets and there, of all people, is Hanama the Assassin. I'm astonished. I didn't really believe she was actually going to be here gambling but there she is. She's wearing a cheap blue robe, the sort of thing worn by your average not-so-well-off Turanian woman on a day out, and she is completely indistinguishable from the rest of the crowd. In fact, with her thin, pale body she looks rather like a schoolgirl who's bunked off for the day to place a bet.

I can't understand it. It's completely unheard of. Assassins dedicate their lives to not having fun. I wonder if she might be here in disguise to assassinate someone. The chariot owners with any luck. I'd be happy to see the owner of Warrior Chief carried out of the Stadium with a knife in his back.

CHAPTER
NINETEEN

'Find out anything?' asks Makri as I return to my seat.

I've never seen her so cheerful. It's really irritating.

'No, I didn't.'

'I expect there's nothing to find out,' says Makri. 'It's just one of those days when the favourites don't come in. Didn't you tell me that happens sometimes? Statistically it's bound to.'

I have twenty gurans on Demon Killer. Makri has thirty on Joyous Sunrise. Joyous Sunrise wins by a length and a half and Makri collects another sixty gurans. Next race I back Venomous Death Adder, the favourite. Makri backs Fairy Rainbow, a rank outsider at twenty-five to one. Fairy Rainbow records its first ever win. Even the charioteer looks surprised. The crowd rises to its feet to protest. The Guards are again obliged to fan out to keep them from invading the track. Bottles and broken chairs rain down on them. I've lost another twenty gurans.

Makri picks up five hundred gurans for her twenty-guran stake and now has the incredible total of one thousand, one hundred and nineteen gurans.

'Easy as bribing a Senator,' she says.

I can't understand it. I've never known anyone be so

successful at the race track simply by backing every chariot with a nice-sounding name.

Honest Mox's son looks glum as he hands over her winnings, though in truth he's doing well. The way the favourites keep losing means he's raking in the public's money. The public is not amused. Only the appearance of the Orcish and Elvish chariots keeps the crowd from staging an uprising. The race officials wisely usher the alien chariots out early knowing that the interest in them will quieten the crowd. It works. As Lord Lisith's chariot appears there is great cheering but when the Orcish chariot rolls out after it there is a tremendous wave of booing and jeering. Frustrations are put to one side as the major race of the day approaches. The Orcish charioteer has long black hair, plaited and tied in a black ribbon. Despite the hostility around him he rides with an air of assurance. I expect he's feeling confident now he has his prayer mat back.

Storm the Citadel comes out next, with Sarija and Kemlath walking behind it. The crowd cheer again. Popular support has brought the odds-on Storm the Citadel down to two to one, the same price as the Elvish Moonlit River. The Orcish chariot, Destroyer, is quoted at four to one. Certain astute punters have been backing it, feeling that a sensible bet is more important than patriotism. Nothing else figures much, the five other chariots in the race being quoted at prices between sixteen to one and eighty to one.

I'm still undecided how to bet. I fancy the Elves to win but I'm not convinced the Orcs won't pull it off. I could do with a nice piece of four to one. I'm down to thirty-two gurans and facing ruin. I delay my bet. The Orcish chariot drifts out to five to one. I'm tempted. I get a strange feeling. It's similar to the one I had down at the warehouse when the Orcs appeared. Nothing strange about that. After all, there are Orcs here.

My senses are picking up something else. A man walks past, a very normal-looking man in a plain tunic and sandals. I notice a slight scar on his forehead. I've never seen him before. Without quite knowing why, I follow him.

He heads up through the terraces. He seems to be in a hurry and I have to use my weight again to keep up. He pays no attention to either the bookmakers or the punters. At the top of the terraces he turns left and makes his way towards the Senators' box. I'm close behind him, still with no idea of why my senses are detecting something unusual.

As he halts in front of the Senators' box I glance at his face. Am I imagining it, or is the scar on his forehead beginning to glow? Cicerius is standing near the front of the box. Right beside him is Lord Rezaz Caseg. I suddenly realise what's happening and make a dive for the stranger. I land on him with all my weight and as we go down a terrific bolt of energy flies straight up in the air. Next second I find myself grappling hand to hand with Makeza the Thunderer. This Orcish Sorcerer is way out of my league in every way, apart from girth. I've prevented the assassination of Rezaz the Butcher, but I might not live to tell the tale.

I have my hands around his neck and I am desperately trying to keep out of the way of the jewel on his forehead. He manages to turn his head enough to send a piercing bolt into my shoulder and I cry out in pain. My spell protection charm has kept me alive, but it's not strong enough to resist a close-range blast of Orcish sorcery.

I yell for help, but the Guards at the Senators' enclosure are slow to react. I remember that I'm carrying my sleep spell. I use it, charging it with as much power as I can. This spell can knock a company of men unconscious, but it has little effect on the powerful Orcish Sorcerer, other than to make him loosen his grip a fraction. I break free, kick him in the ribs, then hurdle the wall into the Senators' enclosure.

'You expect me to do everything?' I gasp, and get myself behind Melus the Fair. Let someone with a bit of power take over.

Makeza the Thunderer, now back in his true form as an Orc Sorcerer, springs to his feet. His eyes are smouldering with fury as he advances. Three Civil Guards leap at him but he brushes them away with a word and they fly through the air. When he comes to the low wall, Makeza doesn't bother to climb. He barks at it and it crumbles before him. Melus the Fair steps in front of him and I'm relieved to notice several other Turanian Sorcerers hurrying to the scene. Makeza isn't going to be easy to beat.

Meanwhile Rezaz the Butcher has drawn his sword in readiness, and so have his attendants. This creates further confusion as the Senators find themselves standing among a group of armed Orcs and aren't quite sure what's going on. The Civil Guards present don't seem to know who they're meant to be protecting. Rezaz steps forward to confront Makeza and the Thunderer immediately releases a powerful blasting spell. The Orc Lord is thrown backwards and slumps to the ground.

Melus spreads her arms and directs all her power against Makeza. She is enveloped by a great burst of yellow light and struggles to free herself. She emerges unscathed and directs a counter-spell at the Thunderer. Again he seems unshaken, and continues to advance towards the prone figure of Rezaz. Two of the Butcher's guards fling themselves in front of the Sorcerer but they too are brushed aside like flies. Another powerful Turanian Sorcerer, Lisutaris, Mistress of the Sky, arrives, but Makeza the Thunderer keeps on coming.

I've seen these Orcish Sorcerers in action before. I know how powerful they can be. Even when Harmon Half-Elf rushes up (with, several losing betting tickets sticking out of his pockets, incidentally) and adds his power to that of Melus and Lisutaris, the issue still seems to be in the balance. Fire crackles through the air and great bolts of lightning strike sparks from the metal railings.

My shoulder hurts. None of my chariots have won. I've lost a lot of gurans. I'm in a really bad mood. If Makeza the Thunderer succeeds in killing Lord Rezaz the Turas Memorial race will be cancelled and I'll never win my money back. I'm completely fed up with this continual disruption at the races. I grab a glass of klee from the hands of a Senator's wife, toss it back, then pick up a heavy chair and start circling around the back of the warring Sorcerers.

A huge maelstrom of fiery colour now envelops most of the Senators' enclosure. I step into the middle of it, offering up a prayer that my charm will protect me. Inside the maelstrom I can't breathe. I grit my teeth and struggle on. Space seems to be warped. I can see Makeza, but he's a long way away. As I struggle forward he takes on the aspect of a huge Orcish war dragon. The dragon turns his long neck towards me, baring its fangs. Through its nose it wears a great ring of power, with a dazzling blue jewel sending out poisonous rays. It reminds me of something, I don't know what. I crash the chair down with all my might on the dragon's head. It disappears with a deafening explosion, and I find myself back in the Senators' enclosure with a broken chair in my hands and an unconscious Orcish Sorcerer at my feet. In front of me Melus the Fair, Lisutaris, Mistress of the Sky, and Harmon Half-Elf are standing in a line looking exhausted. Melus the Fair wipes sweat from her brow.

'It's a long time since I fought an Orc,' she says, breathing heavily. 'For a moment there I thought I was going to be handing in my toga. Nicely done, Thraxas. How did you know that would work?'

'A trick I remembered from the war. When an enemy Sorcerer is fully engaged in sorcerous combat he's often vulnerable to being beaten over the head with a heavy object. Incidentally, I thought that Old Hasius the Brilliant was supposed to be keeping an eye out for Makeza.'

'He's at home with a cold – it's his age,' explains Melus.

Lord Rezaz Caseg struggles to his feet. He thanks the Sorcerers, and me too. It is commonly admitted that it was smart work on my part to recognise Makeza the Thunderer as he walked through the crowd in Human guise.

The congratulations pass me by. I'm a little dazed. Not so much by the battle – the three Sorcerers bore the

brunt of Makeza's attack – but by the sudden inspiration
that hit me when I walked into the magical maelstrom.
I've often found that close involvement with sorcery gets
my intuition working. As soon as I saw the dragon with
its ring of power I realised who killed Senator Mursius.
Foolish of me not to have realised before.

The Senators and their wives troop back into the
enclosure. Consul Kalius looks as if he might be about to
shake my hand, but he thinks better of it and offers me a
stiff thank you instead.

'Don't mention it. Do they sell beer in this enclosure?'

They don't. It's wine only for Senators.

Kalius takes control and issues orders for the races to
resume as quickly as possible, so that the crowd does not
become restive. Makeza the Thunderer is bound and
taken off under heavy sorcerous guard.

I shake my head to clear it, then walk out of the
enclosure, very thoughtful. I find a messenger and hand
him over a small coin to take a note to Captain Rallee.

CHAPTER
TWENTY

'What happened up there?' asks Makri.

'Thraxas once more saves the day for Rezaz the Butcher. I may now be the greatest friend of the Orcs in the west.'

The chariots are lining up behind the tape. I still haven't placed my bet. I can't make up my mind. I notice Hanama in the queue and sneak up behind her. As she reaches the front I strain to hear what she says. It's difficult to make out her soft voice above the noise of the crowd. I think I hear her say Peaceful Dreams of Heaven.

Peaceful Dreams of Heaven is the most useless chariot ever seen in Turai. It was brought in to make up the numbers after a late withdrawal. It was eighty to one at the start of the day and has come in to fifty to one, so a little money must have been placed on it. Not much though. Why would it? It doesn't have a chance.

Hanama disappears into the crowd, gliding easily through the mass of bodies. The trumpets sound for the start of the race. I swallow hard. This goes against the grain.

'Eighteen gurans on Peaceful Dreams of Heaven.'

I rush back to my seat.

'What did you back?' I ask Makri.

'Peaceful Dreams of Heaven,'

'I thought you might,' I say. 'It has a very nice name.'

I glare hard at her. She glares right back at me. The race starts. As the long-awaited contest between the champion chariots of the Orcs and the Elves gets under way the Stadium Superbius explodes with excitement. By the time the chariots reach the first corner not a person is left in their seat. Everyone is up on their feet, screaming encouragement. Not only the ill-behaved masses are carried away. Up in the private enclosure the Senators, Sorcerers and city officials are caught up in the excitement. The Elvish supporters of Lord Lisith are up on their feet waving green banners and the Orcs are standing on their chairs shouting out encouragement in their jagged, guttural language.

For the first time Makri and I have backed the same chariot. Unfortunately it's the worst vehicle in the city. Round the first lap things don't look good. The Elvish Moonlit River has taken an early lead with Sarija's Storm the Citadel close behind. The Orcish Destroyer is going along easily in fourth place. Peaceful Dreams of Heaven is last. Things don't improve much in the second. I scream some abuse at the charioteer. Two chariots collide and another pulls up with a lamed leading horse, leaving Peaceful Dreams fifth out of five going into the third lap.

I can see the Elvish charioteer speaking to his horses, giving them encouragement. The Orcish rider uses his whip. Less kind, but effective, as he moves easily up into third place to lie in wait just behind Storm the Citadel.

The chariot behind the Orcish Destroyer tries to overtake but gets the worst of it when the Orcish charioteer lashes his whip into his opponent's face, sending him crashing into the central barrier. You have to hand it to the Orc, that's good technique. The crowd erupts in a frenzy. As the last lap begins, Moonlit River, Storm the Citadel and Destroyer are nose to tail and going well. The only other remaining chariot, Peaceful Dreams of Heaven, is almost a whole lap behind. I curse myself. I can't believe I put money on this collection of rusted metal and broken-down nags.

'Please send a mighty collision,' I say, raising my eyes briefly to heaven.

Makri is gripped by the madness and seems close to losing control. She's screaming encouragement to Peaceful Dreams and waving her sword in the air, which is illegal in the Stadium, even when your chariot loses.

On the final straight Destroyer makes its move and glides past Storm the Citadel like it was standing still. It draws level with the Elf and they start jostling each other as they come round the bend. The Orcish charioteer lashes his whip at the Elf, who starts lashing him back. Sparks fly as their wheels grind together and the horses hurtle onwards at speeds never before seen in the Stadium. The volume is deafening. I've never seen such madness in a race crowd. Young Sorcerers' Apprentices with whole months' wages staked on the Elf wave their staffs in the air. I see Gurd up on his seat with sweat pouring in torrents down his mighty neck, screaming encouragement.

In the final straight the Elf is ahead by a nose but it seems to me that the Orc is finishing stronger.

'It's all over,' I cry, and hang my head in despair. Suddenly their wheels lock. There is a spectacular collision and both chariots leave the ground. They land in a terrible jumble of Orcs, Elves, wood, metal and horses. Storm the Citadel, racing into the final straight, has no chance. The charioteer tries to pull up but there is no time and he too is thrown into the air as his chariot hits the wreckage and slews across the track.

Peaceful Dreams of Heaven, a long way behind, has plenty of time to slow down and pick its way carefully past the carnage. It trots over the line, the only chariot to complete the race, and the winner. There's a huge collective groan of despair from the crowd. Not in our corner of the crowd, however. Makri goes berserk, and so do I. I practically dance my way down to Honest Mox's to pick up my winnings. I'm as happy as a drunken mercenary. In fact, I'm happier. Eighteen gurans at fifty to one. Nine hundred gurans.

Near Mox's stall an irate mercenary is bemoaning his fate. He's lost all his money and is complaining that the race was fixed.

'Nonsense,' I tell him brusquely. 'Just one of those things. Take it like a man.'

There are some more complaints about the way things have gone but after the incredible excitement of the final race the crowd seems stunned. Most people sit quietly as the race attendants clear away the ruined chariots and give the charioteers some medical attention.

Makri's winnings are almost beyond belief. She has thousands of gurans and has to buy a new bag to carry them. She pulls the coins out in handfuls just to look at them.

I ask her if she'll put it in the track vault for a while.

'What for?'

'I need your help before we go home.'

Captain Rallee taps me on the shoulder. 'Got your message. What's happening?' The Captain has lost all his money and isn't very pleased. 'I'm not convinced this was all fair and square,' he says. 'What do you want?'

'More Civil Guards and a couple of powerful Sorcerers.'

We walk down to the race track. Standing there are Lord Lisith-ar-Moh and Lord Rezaz Caseg, examining the remains of their chariots and checking on the health of their riders and horses. While not exactly friendly, they appear to have reached a truce.

'A fine race.'

'A fine race indeed.'

Sarija is also there. The Elf Lord compliments her politely on the form showed by Storm the Citadel. She replies politely in return, both to Lisith and Rezaz. Melus the Fair appears, along with Kalius and Cicerius. Everyone is polite to everyone else. If the outcome of the race left much to be desired for your average Turanian gambler, in diplomatic terms it was just fine. No one is about to declare war on Turai.

It's a rare moment of peace between Orcs, Elves and Humans. I hate to be the one to spoil the mood but I don't like to drag it out. I walk up to Kemlath Orc Slayer.

'An exciting day, Kemlath. I notice you're wearing your favourite ring. The ring you stole from Senator Mursius when you killed him.'

Captain Rallee looks at me sharply. So do the Consul and the Deputy Consul.

'I suppose it meant something to you, Kemlath, but it was careless of you to take it.' I turn to the Captain. 'That ring belonged to Senator Mursius. And I can prove it. You can see it clearly in the painting of him done after the Orc Wars. It was presented to him by the Consul for bravery.'

Sarija shakes her head, protesting. 'It's Kemlath's ring. The Consul presented them to all the officers.'

I shake my head. 'Afraid not. Kemlath told you that to keep you from suspecting. But I checked the records in the Library. That was the only ring presented by the Consul. Kemlath took it from Mursius because he was jealous of his war record and jealous of you. I've been looking at that painting for days, but it never struck me till now. You know, Kemlath, I wondered why you were paying such close attention to this case. I thought for a while it was just because of your interest in Sarija. But there was more to it than that. You removed the stolen art from the warehouse, but the Society of Friends got there first and took a few items. One of these items was the painting. And you knew you were in trouble if that turned up and someone put two and two together. Like I just did.

'And even if no one connected the ring, the rest of the stolen goods might still incriminate you, because you hadn't had time to clean them all properly. It was smart, sticking close to me. Every time a piece of evidence appeared, like the bronze cup, you sorcerously cleaned all traces of the crime from it. No wonder I drew a blank everywhere I looked.'

Flocks of black stals flop around the track, picking up scraps from the crowd. I never liked these birds.

'The sorcerous messages were going a bit far though. Glixius sent the first and you followed on. You were probably just amusing yourself. Incidentally, you remember that time you told me you detected Glixius's aura on one of them? You never met Glixius. You just made that up. It's funny, really, the way I kept blaming everything on Glixius, when it was you all along.'

Kemlath remains calm. He neither blusters or protests.

'Why would I wish to kill my good friend Mursius?' he says.

'Because you were as jealous as hell of your good friend Mursius for stealing Sarija out from under your nose, that's why. I talked to the old landlady of the Mermaid. You both used to go there during the war when you were stationed on the walls at Twelve Seas. She remembers very well that you asked Sarija to marry you first, and she turned you down for Mursius. I think you've hated him ever since.'

Unruffled, Kemlath continues to deny my accusations.

Captain Rallee is unsure of how to proceed. It's not as if I've produced a cast-iron case, and Kemlath is an important man, another war hero. He looks at Kalius for guidance. Kalius questions me.

'Is the ring all the evidence you have? It seems to me that the ring could have been transferred from Mursius to Kemlath at any time.'

I turn to Sarija. 'Well? Was it?'

She shakes her head. 'Mursius was wearing it the day he disappeared.'

Sarija is wide-eyed with horror. She believes me. There's a woman who'll be deep into her supply of dwa tonight, or maybe sooner. Kalius orders Kemlath's arrest, pending further investigations.

Afterwards Captain Rallee is still troubled. 'Why did he wait twenty years to kill him?'

'I don't really know. Maybe he just brooded on it till it all became too much for him. It might never have happened if he hadn't found himself face to face with Mursius at the warehouse. That was unplanned. Mursius was part of the plot with the Society of Friends to dope the horses. I think Kemlath found out about it and decided to expose him. Unfortunately Sarija chose this time to sell a load of Mursius's art to Axilan, a minor Society of Friends figure, when he was up at the villa collecting the doping plants.

'Kemlath didn't like that. He didn't want anything at the warehouse that might lead to Sarija. If he exposed Mursius, he didn't want Sarija to be arrested as well. So he tried to remove the goods. Unfortunately his visit coincided with Mursius's. I figure Kemlath told Mursius he was going to inform the authorities about the doping and they got into a fight. Kemlath might not have meant to kill him, but that's what happened. It suited him fine anyway. Left him free to woo Sarija.'

Captain Rallee is taking mental notes through all this. He has a powerful memory, the captain. I've never known him forget anything.

'I think you're probably right, Thraxas. But I'm not at all sure we have enough evidence to make it stick in court. Why didn't you wait before denouncing him?'

'Because I was sick of it all, that's why. I've been arrested, made to look foolish and generally given a hard time by everyone. I'm fed up with Kemlath and fed up with the weather and I'm especially fed up with the way the races have gone. I've done my job, I found the killer. If you need more evidence, I'm sure the Guard can dig it up. And now I'm going home.'

'One last thing, Thraxas – the Orcs you said you met down at Ferias, were they for real?'

'Of course! Do you think I'd make that up? They were part of Prince Kalazar's assassination force. Makeza the Thunderer was hiding them there until the race meeting. Probably picked Ferias because the weather was better.'

I walk off. Makri follows me. As we pass Melus they studiously pretend not to know each other.

'Don't bother faking it,' I mutter. 'I know what was going on here today.'

In the landus back to Twelve Seas, Makri plays with her bags of money. I have nine hundred gurans of my own, but now the euphoria of winning has faded I'm in a very bad mood.

'A very fortunate day's gambling,' I say.

'It sure was,' she says, brightly.

'Odd that all those unfancied chariots came in. Very odd. I won nine hundred on the last race. I backed Peaceful Dreams of Heaven even though it was the worst chariot in the race. You want to know why? Because I noticed Hanama betting on it, that's why.'

Makri looks uncomfortable.

'How much of it do you get to keep?' I ask.

'What do you mean?'

'Do you get to spend any of it? Or did you promise to pay it all over to the Association of Gentlewomen?'

'Stop talking rubbish, Thraxas.'

'I'm not talking rubbish. If you're going to tell me that the number three in the Assassins Guild puts on a summer robe and goes to the chariot races for pleasure, I'm not going to believe it. The whole meeting was fixed, Makri, as you well know. And it was nothing to do with the Society of Friends or the Brotherhood. These favourites didn't all break their axles and rear up in fright for no reason. There was sorcery at work there.'

'You can't work sorcery at the Stadium Superbius,' says Makri stubbornly.

'You can if you've recruited the Stadium Sorcerer. You should mention to Melus the Fair that if she wants to pull that scam again she better be a bit more discreet. I know the A.G. needs money in a hurry, but Lilac Paradise a winner? And Peaceful Dreams of Heaven? I figure she picked up some new racing magic on her trip to Samsarina that no one here was familiar with, but if she keeps doing it there will be serious trouble. If the male population of Turai ever finds out that our resident Stadium Sorcerer is casting spells to help win money for the Association of Gentlewomen, they'll tear you all to pieces. And I'll help them.

'I'm disgusted, Makri. I must have seen twenty A.G. supporters in the Stadium, all raking in the money. I wouldn't mind so much if you hadn't tried to throw me off the scent. All that standing around outside my room, talking about betting with Hanama in stage whispers. As if I would think she'd suddenly become interested in the sporting life. She'll end up with a dagger in her back if the Assassins Guild finds out she's spending time working for the Association of Gentlewomen.'

'I guess she's responsible enough to work for who she likes.'

'She's a disgusting killer. So that should suit you well

enough. Who do you think you are, messing around with the races?'

'We need the money,' protests Makri.

'So do all the poor wagon drivers, carpenters and sailors who thought that everything was honest. I tell you, Makri, I'm not pleased. The Stadium Sorcerer cheating the public. Melus the Fair, of all people! I only refrain from denouncing you all to *The Renowned and Truthful Chronicle* because you personally would be thrown off the city walls. The population's had enough of Orcs in the past month. They're not going to take kindly to another one cheating them.'

Makri reacts furiously to this.

'Are you implying that I'm an Orc?'

'Well, you don't have Human values, that's for sure.'

Makri sticks her head out of the landus, yells for the driver to stop, and then leaps out into the street.

'Never speak to me again, you obese drunkard!' she shouts.

'Cheating Orc!' I shout back. She storms off.

'And don't try robbing my room again, pointy ears!' I yell at her departing figure.

The sun is beating down. It's hot as Orcish hell. Even though I've won nine hundred gurans I'm as mad as a mad dragon. I can't stand it that the Association of Gentlewomen outsmarted everyone.

CHAPTER
TWENTY ONE

The city, overstimulated in the past month of discontent, starts to return to normal when the Turas and Triple-Moon Conjunction festivals get under way. The temperature starts to drop as autumn slides into winter.

There was great unhappiness after the race meeting, but surprisingly little suspicion. Everyone trusts Melus the Fair, bless her name. I understand that the Association of Gentlewomen have succeeded in moving their application for Guild status further up the ladder.

Cicerius is pleased with me. The race was run, the Elves still like us and Lord Rezaz will provide protection for the mining territory. If things keep on like this, I may get back to the Palace one day.

The Civil Guards dig more deeply into Kemlath's role in the death of Mursius and succeed in building a reasonable case against him. Even Captain Rallee admits that I was sharp as an Elf's ear on this one.

Kemlath doesn't come to trial however. Unless it's a case of high treason any citizen as important as Kemlath, especially one who was a hero in the war, is usually given the opportunity to flee the city before going to court. A member of the aristocracy is most unlikely to face the scaffold, or a long spell in the prison galleys. Instead they retire into exile, which Kemlath does.

Sarija remains in the city, spending her inheritance on dwa. Glixius Dragon Killer sends me a message. He likes me even less than before and will kill me at the first opportunity. Given the way I mistakenly harried him over the Mursius case, I can't exactly blame him.

At least I picked up nine hundred gurans at the races, and won't have to work for a while. That's the only bright spot on the horizon. With winter around the corner I'd like to spend a few months just sitting in the warmth of the Avenging Axe with my feet up, drinking beer. Unfortunately Makri makes it impossible for me to relax.

'I've never seen her this mad,' says Tanrose.

Gurd nods his agreement.

'Yesterday she damned near demolished the wall out the back with her axe. Said she was practising fighting, but I noticed she'd chalked a picture of you on it, Thraxas. Why did you call her an Orc?'

'We were arguing.'

As no one else in Turai seems to realise that the Association of Gentlewomen fixed the races I've decided that I'm not going to be the one to expose them. Partly I'm concerned for Makri's safety. Also there might be attempts to take back the nine hundred gurans I won. But I'm still as mad as hell at Makri. She can chop down as many pictures of me as she likes, I refuse to apologise. Cheating at the Turas Memorial is despicable behaviour. Even Astrath Triple Moon confined his larceny to the minor meetings.

Makri appears from the street outside.

'Come for your evening shift?' says Gurd.

She shakes her head. 'I'm leaving. I refuse to live in the same tavern as a fat useless drunk who called me an Orc.' She storms upstairs.

'What are you looking at me for?' I demand. 'How come I'm the one that always has to apologise around here? You heard what she called me.'

'Come on, Thraxas. You know you should make up. You'd hate it if Makri really left. Who'll protect your back when you go up against these villains?'

'I managed to protect my own back just fine before she came along. Let her leave. She annoys the hell out of me anyway. If it's not that damned women's group then it's some stupidity she's picked up from Samanatius the Philosopher. Who ever heard of a Barbarian from the east going to the Guild College anyway? The whole thing is ridiculous.'

Gurd and Tanrose continue to look at me accusingly. I start to feel persecuted.

'Well goddamn it, if it means that much to the pair of you, I'll say I'm sorry. Not that it'll do any good. Even Makri isn't naive enough to fall for a bunch of flowers three times in a row.'

On two previous occasions when Makri was apparently irreconcilably annoyed at me I had given her a bunch of flowers, at the suggestion of Tanrose. It seemed like a lousy way of apologising to me but it had a spectacular effect on Makri. She burst into tears and ran out of the room in fact. Both times. Tanrose put it down to her growing up in a gladiator slave pit and never really getting any presents before.

Makri appears downstairs with a bag over her shoulder.

'And tell that corpulent slug if he buys me flowers I'll ram them down his throat,' she says, storming out of the door.

'She's just saying that,' says Tanrose. 'I'm sure it would work again.'

I stare at her in amazement. Tanrose seems to have an almost mystical belief in the power of a small bunch of flowers. It's ridiculous.

'Buy her a new axe,' suggests Gurd. 'I think she damaged her favourite one hacking down the wall.'

Which is why I find myself tramping through Quintessence Street and up to the market on my way to the armourer's. The weather is pleasant, with the warm autumn air showing the first sign of cooling. Winter is not far away. Winter in Turai is hell. I'm really going to regret it if I can't spend it comfortably in front of a roaring fire at the Avenging Axe.

I reach the armourer. There's a sign on it saying: 'Closed due to bereavement'. I forgot that the armourer's third son was killed in a crossbow incident last week. The fourth son is due in court any day now.

It's too late to reach another armourer. It'll have to wait till tomorrow. I make my way back into Quintessence Street. I buy a pastry from the bakery. Minarixa is less friendly than usual. Probably Makri has been spreading bad stories about me.

I stop in the street to eat.

'Come for some flowers?' says Baxos the flower seller.

'Hey, Rox,' he calls over to the fish vendor. 'Thraxas is buying flowers again.'

'Still got his lady friend, has he?' yells back Rox, loud enough for the entire street to hear.

'You treat her nicely, Thraxas!' screams Birix, one of Twelve Seas' busiest prostitutes.

I glare at Baxos and toss him a coin just to get away. I arrive back in the Avenging Axe holding a large bunch of flowers.

'I thought you were buying an axe?'

'The axe shop was shut.'

It sounds a bit lame. I thrust the flowers into Makri's hand. My hand strays to my sword, just in case she gets violent.

Makri raises the flowers to dash them to the ground. Suddenly a tear trickles from her eye. She refrains from dashing them to the ground and instead rushes forward, embraces me then runs out of the room in tears. I'm unsure of what this means.

'Did it work again?'

'Of course,' says Tanrose.

I can't understand it. Neither can Gurd.

'This is a woman who once fought a dragon. She killed a nine-foot Troll when she was thirteen.'

Tanrose shrugs. 'I imagine it was really grim growing up where she did. There's obviously a lot of mileage left in small presents where Makri is concerned.'

Gurd snorts. 'The women in my village were not like that. It took at least a new plough to impress them.'

'That must be why you never married,' says Tanrose. 'You should have ignored the ploughs and tried flowers.'

She looks rather pointedly at Gurd. He seems embarrassed. He's been attracted to Tanrose for a long time, but any mention of the subject makes him uneasy. These northern Barbarians. No romance. I leave them to it.

Upstairs I check on my supplies. I need plenty of klee

and thazis to get me through the winter. And maybe some new blankets. I have nine hundred gurans. Enough for plenty of thick blankets. I might even buy one for Makri. She doesn't have much money and she handed over all her winnings to the A.G. Foolish behaviour, it seemed to me, but that's the problem with being idealistic. It makes you do foolish things. Personally, I'd have kept every guran.

THRAXAS

Martin Scott

In the magical city of Turai, murder, mayhem and
ruthless criminal brotherhoods are rife. The only
people more corrupt than the politicians are the
Royal Family. And the weather is awful.

It's down these mean, muddy streets that Thraxas,
ex-soldier, failed Sorcerer and epic drinker, ekes out
a living as a Private Investigator.

But when Princess Du-Akai, third in line to the
throne, asks him to investigate a very delicate matter,
it seems that his luck is about to change. And it does.
A few hours later, he's in jail accused of murder.

Thraxas is a new star of comic fantasy. A man of
extraordinary courage, legendary strength and
nerves of steel he isn't, but his unique charm and
very well-hidden talents are destined to make him
one of the best-loved characters in fantasy fiction.

THRAXAS AND THE
WARRIOR MONKS

Martin Scott

It's summer in the magical city of Turai and it's hotter than Orcish hell. All that Thraxas, third-rate sorcerer, second-rate private investigator and first-rate layabout, is looking for is a bit of peace and quiet. But when one of his clients is arrested in his office for murder, even Thraxas has to act.

It should be a simple enough case. So why do rival bands of warrior monks keep turning up? And how did a life-size bronze statue of Saint Quatinius disappear into thin air? And what's all this got to do with the dolphins and their lost healing stone?

Before long, Thraxas and his friends find themselves at the heart of another incredible case of sorcerous skullduggery and magical mayhem.

OPEN SESAME

Tom Holt

Something was wrong! Just as the boiling water was about to be poured on his head and the man with the red book appeared and his life flashed before his eyes, Akram the Terrible, the most feared thief in Baghdad, knew that this had happened before. Many times. And he was damned if he was going to let it happen again. Just because he was a character in a story didn't mean that it always had to end this way.

Meanwhile, back in Southampton, it's a bit of a shock for Michelle when she puts on her Aunt Fatima's ring and the computer and the telephone start to bitch at her. But that's nothing compared to the story that the kitchen appliances have to tell her . . .

Once again, Tom Holt, the funniest and most original of all comic fantasy writers, is taking the myth.

'Tom Holt stands out on his own . . . If you haven't read any Tom Holt, go out and buy one now. At least one. But don't blame me for any laughter-induced injuries'
Vector

<u>WISH YOU WERE HERE</u>

Tom Holt

It was a busy day on Lake Chicopee. But it was a mixed bunch of sightseers and tourists that had the strange local residents rubbing their hands with delight.

There was Calvin Dieb, the lawyer setting up a property deal, who'd lost his car keys.

There was Linda Lachuk, the tabloid journalist who could smell that big, sensational story.

There was Janice DeWeese, who was just on a walking holiday but who longed for love.

And finally, but most promising of all, there was Wesley Higgins, the young man from Birmingham, England, who was there because he knew the legend of the ghost of Okeewana. All he had to do was immerse himself in the waters of the lake and he would find his heart's desire. Well, it seemed like a good idea at the time.

Welcome to Lake Chicopee!
Welcome to your Heart's Desire!
And enter the amazing world of Tom Holt's
new comic masterpiece.

101 DAMNATIONS

Andrew Harman

So, there's this dragon. Well, it's not a real dragon,
more of a, um, virtual dragon. The Thaumaturgical
Physicists of Losa Llamas want it as security. Their
real mistake was employing Cheiro Mancini, alchemist
and Virtual Ecology Technician (VET for short), to
install it. I mean, if it wasn't for him the Scroles
wouldn't have been disturbed, and the Damnations
would have stayed under control, and as for the
Prime Evil . . .

In *101 Damnations*, Andrew Harman introduces a
whole new set of characters to the twin kingdoms of
Rhyngill and Cranachan – and proves that they are
just as incompetent as his previous heroes!

IT CAME FROM ON HIGH

Andrew Harman

It's never easy addressing a crowd. Especially when
the crowd is going to be the entire world – live – and
you're stuck for inspiration. And after the scientific
proof that the Turin Shroud is real proves too
convoluted for Pope Joshua Angeles to use, it seems that
the only sensible course of action is to panic. However,
when he hears that something has fallen
from the sky, destroying the Chapel of St Tib's, he
suddenly becomes very inspired. Unfortunately,
so do the US Military and the Secret Services of
every major world power.

And, to make matters worse, the angry parents of
two eloping aliens have appeared at the edge of the
solar system. Joshua soon realises that it'll take a
miracle to save the planet. It's a good thing, then,
that the Church has a fair bit of experience in the
miracle department.

At last – the Truth the Vatican couldn't tell!
Read all about it in Andrew Harman's dazzling
new comic fantasy.

Orbit titles available by post:

❏ Thraxas	Martin Scott	£5.99
❏ Thraxas and the Warrior Monks	Martin Scott	£5.99
❏ Open Sesame	Tom Holt	£5.99
❏ Wish You Were Here	Tom Holt	£5.99
❏ 101 Damnations	Andrew Harman	£5.99
❏ It Came From On High	Andrew Harman	£5.99

The prices shown above are correct at time of going to press. However, the publishers reserve the right to increase prices on covers from those previously advertised, without further notice.

ORBIT

ORBIT BOOKS
Cash Sales Department, P.O. Box 11, Falmouth, Cornwall, TR10 9EN
Tel +44 (0) 1326 372400, Fax: +44 (0) 1326 374888
Email: books@barni.avel.co.uk

POST AND PACKING:
Payments can be made as follows: cheque, postal order (payable to Orbit Books) or by credit cards. Do not send cash or currency.

U.K. orders under £10	£1.50
U.K. orders over £10	**FREE OF CHARGE**
E.C. & Overseas	25% of order value

Name (Block letters) ....

Address ....

....

Post/zip code: ....

☐   Please keep me in touch with future Orbit publications

☐   I enclose my remittance £ ....

☐   I wish to pay by Visa/Access/Mastercard/Eurocard

Card Expiry Date